SETRA THE SEA TROUT

&

OTHER STORIES

Charles Bingham.

Dedicated to my grandchildren: Freddie, Charlotte, Clementine, Jonathan, Oliver and Alexandra, who all listened to my bedtime stories.

SETRA THE SEA TROUT

&

OTHER STORIES

Charles Bingham

EXCELLENT PRESS

Ludlow

First published in 2010 by
Excellent Press
9 Lower Raven Lane
Ludlow
Shropshire
SY8 1BL

British Library Cataloguing in Publication Data
A catalogue entry of this book is available from
the British Library.

ISBN 978-1-900318-42-6

Printed in Great Britain by
TJ International Ltd

Acknowledgements

The author thanks the many flyfishers and Westcountry characters who have, unwittingly, been the subjects of some of the stories in this book. In particular, the late Gilbert Warne, known as Penrose in the story of that name, doyen salmon flyfisher of the West Dart river.

Thanks are due to the Duchy of Cornwall which keeps the river Dart open to all flyfishers above Dartmeet, and to John Fogden and Bob Beard, who provided, and provide, me with fishing on the lower river. Bill and Jane Robertson, stalwarts of the Dart Fisheries Association Secretariat, deserve the thanks of all for their dedicated work and reports. Luke Chester-Master made available his ancient shepherd's hut as a refuge at the water's edge.

I thank Jonathan Young, editor of *The Field*, for permission to reprint the *Adventures of a Sea Trout*, and Paul Knight, Chief Executive of the Salmon and Trout Association, for similarly allowing republication of *Giles and the Ancient Dartmoor Trout* from the Association's magazine.

Special acknowledgement is made of the help of split cane flyfisher and publisher of this, and two of my earlier books, David Burnett.

The painting on the jacket is by Robin Armstrong. The engravings were made by Julian Waterman in 1988 while an undergraduate at Oxford University.

Contents

Setra the Sea Trout

CHAPTER 1

The Estuary

SETRA RESTED AT the mouth of the Tors river after the final day of his migration from Land's End along the underwater marine paths followed by generations of sea trout. Three times he had swum the length of the river to the finger streams on the moor. There, in past spawnings, he had fertilized with his milt the ova extruded by females in gravel redds. Setra had watched them work, curving their bodies in spasms to force the eggs from their vents; he then lay alongside, ejecting his sperm upon the ova. On each homeward sea journey when entering the estuary in spring, he tasted traces of fresh water which had run down from the upland streams of nativity. The flavours of peat, and water stains from heather flanked marshes, spewed widely from the river mouth into the sea.

Swinging north between the port and starboard buoys of the main channel Setra swam to the top of the narrowing seaway. For two hours the sea trout waited, poised half an inch above the bed of sand piled up in front of a car engine block. The block, dropped by fishermen as anchor to a mooring chain, was encrusted with limpets and trailing seaweed. The links no longer secured a fishing boat because the chain which had attached it to an oil drum, floating as a buoy upon the surface, had rusted free and lay in twisted abandon on the sand. Setra's tail moved slightly, two or three inches in front of the engine, as the peal took account of shifts in the water current slicing by on the ebb tide. His tail was grey, broad and convex at the trailing edge where it became thin as parchment, before narrowing to the wrist where the rays of gristle entered the scale clad muscle of the body. The tail dispensed his power. In front of the dorsal fin the scales on both flanks had been stripped in two thin light coloured lines reaching from the darkness of his back to the pale belly. These lines were the scrape marks left when the tail had driven his seven pound body through a hole in an estuary sweep net. Setra had escaped upstream leaving the scales on the broken threads and knots. Five sea lice, each the size and shade of a woodlouse, clung by suckers to his skin in the shelter of the dorsal fin, and three more were outlined against the flank above the anal fin. Setra dropped back a foot and twisting his body rubbed the lice against the block—the lice clung on but the metal roughened the front of the anal fin. He returned to his position ahead of the block, waiting for the flood tide which would arrive to deepen the brackish water over the sand bars and provide cover from the seals. With the tide he would swim to the salmon ladder on the weir which divided the Tors river from the tidal waters of the sea.

After two hours the ebb slackened and, no longer feeling the need of the engine which had buttressed him against the seaward flow, Setra swam forward slowly in the slack tide. A small lobster, who had a refuge in one of the rusted cylinder holes of the block, crept out cautiously on thin jointed legs behind two seeking feelers. The lobster had crouched in the back of the hole as Setra's tail waved in front of him throughout the afternoon. Now, with daylight fading in the unknown void above the sea, the tail had gone and the lobster emerged in search of food, the unwanted fish and offal thrown from the fishing boats which anchored in the bay. Other boats were tied up alongside the timber baulks lining the quay side, the spliced loops of their mooring warps dropped over cast iron bollards set on bolts cemented into slabs of stone. The boats rocked idly on the waves which, ebbing and swelling, pressed them against old car and lorry tyres suspended as buffers between their topsides and the quay. The scene, the shadows and the stillness were illuminated by street lamps whilst the town slept when Setra swam by.

The sea trout drifted on, carried forward by the flood tide. Trailers of sea weed, anchored to the rocks, now pointed with the current to the river. Setra swam a little faster than the salt water flowing in over the sand bars, then increased his effort as he entered the shallower ripple where fresh water predominated and flowed against him between the banks. He passed beneath a road bridge spanning the river where it met the sea, and accelerated as a lorry thundered and vibrated overhead. The river banks now sloped down into black mud which was covered and uncovered by the ebbs and flows of the tide. Tin cans, plastic containers, rubber boots and discarded flotsam rested on the mud which was the hunting ground of gulls, small green crabs and the night time rats of the estuary town.

Setra continued upstream to a wide pool of deep water bounded at the top by a weir of stone. At one end of the weir the river flowing to the sea was channelled down a salmon ladder of small pools, each eighteen inches above the next. The water cascaded through narrow gaps, swirling and bubbling at each level to obscure a watcher's view of stones and sodden logs resting on the bottom, and distorting the shapes of passing fish. The sea trout edged up to the entrance to the ladder, tested the water strength and felt the depth, swam around the sea pool twice then settled fifteen yards below the lowest step to wait at the end of the current for rain to fall in the hills and increase the flow down the valley. When that time arrived he would jump the first step to thrust and force his way up each stage to the river.

Shortly after dawn the town stirred, people appeared, old men exercised dogs on the open spaces, and cars and buses shook the riverside road. Craak the heron, who had been stalking frogs in the rushes since first light, was disturbed and took to the air with a harsh cry, beating up and away on broad grey wings to the heronry where his three ragged feather sprouting youngsters waited for food in the tree top nest. The heronry of four flat nests of sticks occupied the highest branches of an oak tree which grew out of moss and lichen covered mounds, sole remaining evidence of a monastery reduced at the Dissolution. The parent acorn of the oak had been dropped two centuries after this disturbance by a jackdaw which had perched on one of the crumbling walls. Losing interest in the seed the jackdaw had watched the acorn tumble onto the ground, his grey head cocked to one side. He then forgot about his plaything and strutted off along the wall to hunt for beetles in the crevices. The acorn had germinated, sending a white root down between the blocks of stone to reach the earth, and upwards it thrust a shoot which sprouted green leaves. Two hundred years later the oak reached its present size before, in senility, commencing a slow decline. Two heavy branches rotted on the ground below the tree and these and the scant grass were splashed with white droppings having a fishy smell from the overhead nests.

As the heron's shadow swept over the water Setra's fins and tail ceased all movement, pointing stiffly from his body which tensed, poised for flight. Returning to a state of torpid relaxation, his skin soothed by the water sliding by, he lost awareness of time.

Carrying a fishing rod an angler in black rubber boots walked along the riverside path, turned in opposite the base of the weir and moved to the water's edge where the river disgorged from the ladder into the sea pool. He stood on a flat rock, the surface of which had been smoothed by anglers over the years, and peered into the water. Taking a rusty tobacco tin from his jacket he extracted a pink prawn to which was bound a length of nylon with a treble hook tied to the end. The hook was concealed in the prawn's whiskers where there was no saw edged spear on the head, for the man had snapped it off believing the sharp spike would deter a salmon. He knotted the nylon trace, together with a weight, to the end of the line coming from the reel through the rings of the rod. Balancing himself, his legs widespread on the flat rock, he cast the prawn to the side of the current, raised the rod tip and felt the weight trundle over the bedrock of the pool.

Setra regarded the prawn without alarm as it swung across in front of him. He was untroubled by its presence for he knew them to be harmless prey if gripped across the body. He was not hungry. The feeding at sea had been good for several months, oil and fat swelled the pink flakes of his muscles and he would feed no more until the following

January when, after spawning in the headwaters of the river in December, he would return to the sea. The man pulled up the bait and drawing more line from the reel swung out the prawn two yards further down the pool. The prawn drifted towards Setra's tail and he eased forward six feet, being uneasy at all times of anything approaching to his rear. A large rainbow trout, escaped product of an up-river trout farm, inspected the prawn, swirling and pushing it with his nose. The trout was hungry. Having been swept down river on a spate the week before, it missed the meals of fish pellets which had been thrown to it daily by the farmer. The rainbow took the prawn and the angler, registering a tension on the line, struck upwards with the rod. The hooked trout ran for the darkness of the rocks beneath the weir but was overcome by the pressure of the line, drawn up to the flat rock and netted. The man was disappointed, having hoped for a salmon to sell to the fishmonger in the town, but he knocked the trout on the head and, slipping it into the lining of his jacket, reeled up his line and walked away in the direction from which he had come.

Setra waited on in torpor for several days, the prawns and spinning baits of other anglers regularly moved close to him but he ignored them. He was joined daily on the flood tides by salmon, also on their spawning run. The salmon investigated the sea pool on arrival for this was, for most of them, their first and only journey up the river. Salmon died and were broken up by the heavy waters of the winter river after they had laid and fertilized their eggs. At times they circled close to the bottom of the pool, following each other; occasionally one dropped back, accelerated hard, fast and up to fling himself in glittering abandon through the mirror of the water surface film. Small boys who passed by after school gaped at this spectacle of power and returned later with youth's fishing outfits—the telephone wires and other cables crossing the river were festooned with their floats, hooks and shrivelled worms.

With the passing of seven days there had gathered in the pool eighteen salmon, of weights between seven and twenty-three pounds, and four large sea trout of which Setra was the heaviest. The flooding sea water was now raised higher each day with the advent of spring tides, and the fish became restless in their desire for rainfall and a rising river in spate to coincide with the lunar tidal increase which would enable them to run the ladder. Setra opened and closed his mouth, tasting the water on his tongue for the stains and traces of moorland peat, first signals of a coming flood. The magnet of the river and the spawning redds pulled at him; the sperm forming in his awakening milt sacs made him restless to continue his up-river journey.

CHAPTER 2

Pengelly catches a Salmon

PENGELLY SAT OPPOSITE me on 25 March in the living room of his cottage on the Tors moor. Born on a nearby farm he had retired to live in familiar surroundings, subsiding with a sigh of content into the folds and valleys between the heather covered hills. His stubby eyebrows reminded me of the grey lichens firmly attached to granite rocks, and his side whiskers were like moss growing on the trunks of gnarled beech trees. Like the beech trees Pengelly was thick waisted and impervious to the moorland rain. Born into a family of moormen of independent minds but little wealth, for the acid upland soils yielded a sparse return on the labours of the stockman and the shepherd, the younger sons left home for the army, to read law or qualify in other professions. Pengelly had become a vet, leaving university to practise in what he called the softer side of Devon to the east of Exeter. After his retirement he had come back to the moor to pursue interests close to his heart in a style unhampered by convention. The chair on which he now rested was low, and his leather-slippered feet obtained no great purchase on the carpet as he struggled to lean forward to poke the logs glowing on a pile of grey wood ash in the granite fireplace below a mantelpiece of rough-hewn oak. Life was overtaking him I knew, but at seventy-eight years of age he had the wisdom to pick out the better moments and with a twinkling eye enjoy them to the full. Ten years back he had thought nothing of covering several miles of river bank over the rough moor rod in hand, searching with his fly each likely salmon lie, the short bent body rolled along the waterside by gum booted stumpy legs. As he aged he watched the water conditions more closely, fished when the time was right, husbanded his strength. One day it would all be over and life would end, but as he said to me "I want one more salmon—just one will do this year". He had been saying this each spring for the past three seasons and it meant little for the river always drew him back.

Pressing with his hands upon the arms of the upholstered chair he levered himself to his feet, moved across the room and sat on a wooden bench below the window. He peered beyond the few feet of garden to the hills and folds which were hidden in the distance by passing banks of light grey rain. He loved that open view, broken by the stark leafless branches of stunted blackthorn bushes outlined against the sky. In winter evenings when the curtains were drawn he looked instead at the watercolour above the fireplace: the painting was of a moorland valley of the East Okemont river, a scene which had been carried to paper by the brush of Widgery, late mayor of Exeter. The painted stream, for that was all it was so high in the hills, was enclosed by peat and heather covered banks of brown and mauve. Pengelly enjoyed the picture on those evenings as he tied his salmon flies at the pine table set to one side of the room. He worked by the light of a Tilley lamp, having no electricity, for the mains were not available to so isolated a house and he felt the noise of a thumping diesel generator would be a pollution of the silence of the moor. Of course it was only silent to those who could not hear with understanding, had not been taught wild sounds or learned to listen. In winter he heard the two-tone whistle of the golden plover, the lapwing's cry and the scream of the mating fox. Spring brought the isolated call of nesting curlews, and deep-throated ravens passed across the sky. Pengelly would not consider living elsewhere in his final years and as he had no one to please but himself, his wife having died when he was seventy, he would, as he said, turn up his toes just where he pleased.

I knew he had a married daughter living on a farm near Plymouth for she visited him each Wednesday, driving a Land Rover up the bumpy track over the moor to the cottage. She brought him small comforts, steak and kidney pies which she had prepared and baked, and chided him if he had forgotten to change his shirt or the sheets upon the bed. When alone he ate frugally, brown wholemeal bread, cheese and apples, trout in season from the streams, and the pigeons and rabbits he shot from time to time. He was not a man to say "I've had enough", to become tired of life, though he did once admit that it would not be his wish to go through it all again. Although he reminisced when I called for a cup of tea his life was still active and versatile: a puppy, a hive of bees, home made wine—all were encompassed. A quarter century older than myself I admired the clear view he took of life and the vein of perception in his observations, but there was no doubt that he was slowly failing. "My joints are wearing out" he paused, thought, and continued "but I daresay they'll do another season". The statement was not made with open regret, it was just a fact, unalterable, and he would make the most of what he had.

The rain outside became a little heavier, obscuring the wooden gate two hundred yards distant beside which grew a mountain ash: the tree and gate marked the track he took to fish the upper reaches of the Tors river. In the autumn this rowan would produce bunches of red berries which Pengelly gathered, visiting other trees as well until he had a basketful to make a special jelly. It was his practice to keep the little pots with their burgundy coloured contents in case he shot a hare.

A roast golden plover benefited from the jelly and the plover was just about enough for one. "If it goes on raining like this for a few more hours we could go to the lower river above Tormouth tomorrow" he stated. "Water would be a bit coloured, but the spate is bound to bring up a few fish". I left him after finishing my tea, with the promise to call in my car at ten o'clock in the morning to drive him the fifteen miles to the lower river. Pengelly returned to the fireside chair, shook off his slippers and stretched his feet towards the flames. His circulation was not as good as it used to be and his feet at times grew cold. Raising himself he moved across the room to the dresser where he poured a tot of whisky from the decanter before returning to the fire. He sipped the whisky, felt the spirit burn his chest, and soon his feet grew warm. He thought about the next day, the rod he would take and whether he ought to tie a fly or two. His thoughts slowed, his chin rested on his chest, and he dozed in the comfort of content.

Later he took down the salmon fly rod from its resting place on pegs along the wall. It was of spliced cane in three four-foot sections. These lengths were bound together with insulating tape for he rarely took the rod apart, mounting it on the roof of the car on clips attached to the gutters. The reel, a Hardy Perfect, clicked sweetly as he turned the drum which revolved smoothly on the oiled ball race. The fly box caused some consternation after the winter storage. "Bliddy varmints" he exclaimed, lapsing into the local dialect which he used when put out by some unexpected factor. The moth had been inside, ravaging the feathers, and whether he liked it or not he would have to dress a brace of flies for the next day. He pulled open the drawer of the pine table and took out his fly tying vice, clamped it to the table top and set a hook in the jaws. With a reel of black silk, tufts of red dyed hair from the tail of a deer, silver tinsel and lead wire he constructed a fly, mulling over the colours, satisfying his ideas, and sealing the head with black varnish. It was a rewarding task, simple and comforting to his practiced fingers. He looked at the lure with pleasure, confident that it was better than the overdressed patterns sold in shops. A salmon would take his fly in preference to any other if in the mood. That depended on so many things: the height of the water, its temperature and colour, and whether the birds had started to sing. Pengelly always fished harder when the thrushes sang in the spring. The warming afternoon sunshine stimulated the birds, early large olive flies hatched, and then a salmon might stir to take his lure. Yes, there was no doubt that one should fish harder when the birds sang. He tied two more flies which he placed in a tin with a spool of nylon, leaving the tin, his net and waders by the back door ready for the morning. He lit a candle, screwed out the lamp and mounted the creaking wooden stairs to bed. He slept fitfully, his mind returning to the excitement of the morning when he would fish for the first time after the short days and long lonely nights of winter.

Outside the cottage on the other side of the yard, Whiteface sat on the roof of the empty stables. At one time, when Pengelly kept a horse, there had been a plentiful supply of mice with holes and runs in the buildings. The mice had bored into the wooden oat bins and the owl had fed on them. Now that the horse had gone, riding being beyond the old man's stiffened joints, the owl hunted the dried-up grasses of the moor for voles and field mice. His mate had laid their first white egg on a nest by disgorged pellets in the stable loft where both of them roosted on a beam by day. Pengelly broke open the pellets from time to time to examine the undigested fur and shiny white teeth of mice, the hard wingcases of beetles and the bones of frogs. When his mate hatched her clutch in June Whiteface would be forced to hunt by day as well as night to feed his offspring—Pengelly often saw the buff-coloured bird floating over the moor and waited, expectant, for it to turn sharply in a twisting dive upon an unsuspecting vole. Whiteface bobbed his head, gave a shriek, which was answered by his mate in the rowan tree towards the river, and took off on silent soft-feathered wings.

When I called for Pengelly the following morning the rain had cleared, the clouds had lifted and larks rose in the blue sky to sing to the rising sun and their nesting mates. From the window of his living room I could see the rowan tree by the gate and the river beyond which snaked out from behind a hill to the right, widened into the Stone Cross pool before disappearing to the south on the far side of a wood of stunted beech trees. The Stone Cross pool was where Pengelly fished for salmon and sea trout in the back end of the season on August days and nights. In September he only fished by day for the nights grew darker and darker and in recent years his sight had dimmed and the step of his foot become less sure. He did not want to fall to lie alone amongst the granite rocks.

We drove down the valley road which led to Tormouth, crossing and re-crossing the river on narrow stone bridges. As the car dropped from the moors towards the sea the country softened: peat, granite and heather gave way to red sandstone soil, green fields and the gentler broad-leaved woods. We left behind the shaggy Galloway cattle of the uplands and passed instead short-coated Devons. Pengelly craned his neck at each river crossing and reported what he saw—he was encouraging for the river ran dark but clear. He called out that the rocks of the river bed were visible and the flow was white at the waterfalls where it broke in spray.

I parked the car at the end of a track between meadows, Pengelly unclipped the rod from the roof of the car, we put on waders and I carried the lunch in a game bag to the waterside. I would not fish, being satisfied by the thought that my companion might try the likely places. The nests of rooks were in the riverside trees; I looked up at them, noting those which were new and lighter in colour than the ones which had withstood the winter gales. The cawing of the rooks changed from dreamy caas to a raucous alarm at the sight of my pale upturned face and staring eyes. Pengelly tied on his fly, drew line from the reel and began to fish. He cast across the pools and paid attention to flat unrippled places which marked the positions of rocks on the river bed. He was absorbed, and if I didn't look at him but let my eyes relax to encompass the wider scene he disappeared, his tweed clothes blending into the bank and bushes from which they only became outlined when I focused on him. A dipper bird flew down the river, alighted on a boulder close to the tail of the pool and bobbed his white waistcoat, jerking up and down on the water-sprayed rock before entering the river to hunt the shallows for tadpoles, caddis larvae and other creeping things. The dipper had a nest under the railway bridge five hundred yards upstream where his mate sat still and silent on five white eggs.

The old man moved on down the river to Monk's Pool and began to fish where the monks in years gone by operated a fish trap. His line rolled out to drop the fly close to the far bank and he at once switched the line upstream in a mend to ensure the fly swam slowly across the river until it hung in the current downstream of his rod. Setra watched the fly from his lie in front of a slab of rock which had once formed part of the fish trap which had crumbled over the ages. The night before he had jumped and swum the salmon ladder on the rising water to make his way upstream the five miles to Monk's Pool where he arrived soon after daybreak. He rested now in the fresh water and watched the shining surface mirror above his head. He had paused in front of the stone slab two years previously and many salmon had occupied the lie since the stone had fallen from the fish trap wall. The eight sea lice still clung to his scales but they felt uncomfortable in the fresh water and would drop off with the passing of two more days. One of the salmon with whom he had spent the waiting time in the sea pool moved alongside Setra to share the ease of the lie; this salmon weighed eleven pounds and had followed the sea trout in the ladder ascent and up the river trail. Setra shifted over, his left flank protected by the wall, whilst to his right the salmon waited for the next night when both would swim again towards the moor. Pengelly had caught many salmon over the years from the fish trap lie. He worked his fly down with care, bringing the red bucktail lure across the front of the fish, dangling it in temptation, exciting it with little jerks. Setra had seen these things before, he was old and wise in the ways of glittering fishlets which were not fishlets, which moved enticingly in the water; they had a strange power which pulled at the mouth. He ignored the fly. The salmon became disturbed by the fly thing which moved closer to him, he sank back on the current, then rose in a fast turn to investigate. Pengelly saw the momentary lightening of the river colour by the stone as the salmon turned, he drew in the line, hooked up the fly on the rod butt and sat down on a stump. He took an apple from his pocket and ate it slowly, spitting out the pips. An apple gave a salmon time to settle. He dropped the core into the centre of the rotten stump, stood up and cast again. I could tell that something was up for I knew the place and Pengelly. I did not speak. He false cast twice, then sent the line across the river where the fly plopped in, his eyes tense beneath the lichen brows and his thick calloused fingers tender on the line, feeling for the take. And then he raised his head and the rod tip bent and the salmon broke surface in a startled leap as the hook drove home.

Later we admired the silver form on the freshness of the grass, the back was dark, the flanks firm and sea lice clung on unaware that their chance of life was gone.

Pengelly was glad that our journey had not been fruitless but he was also sad. He could not do what the fish had done, swim there and back across the Atlantic to feed near Greenland, navigate the ocean currents, slip up the river ways. The end of life was final and he had been the cause.

Setra waited. For a time he had followed the fighting salmon, swimming behind the struggling fish, curious and distressed. He then hid in the deep of the pool to wait for the protection of the night.

CHAPTER 3

Setra's Passage to Brock Weir

DURING THE EVENING of 26 March, after Pengelly had left the river, the wind changed from west to north east: a bitter wind, dry, cold and hard. Gusts rocked the rook nests in the treetops upstream of Monk's Pool, causing the sitting hens to settle low in the grass-lined cups whilst gathering close their treasured clutches of mottled green eggs. The males clung to the swaying branches in the night, pointing their beaks into the eye of the gale, their plaintive caas of discomfort and dismay swept away by the buffeting wind. A nest built with sure support against the prevailing westerlies was unable to withstand the changed direction and tumbled down from branch to branch, bounced off the trunk and dropped into the river. The cracked eggs left stains of orange yolk on the rushes where an eel, which had taken up residence under the bank, gorged on one whole egg and the remnants of others which dripped and trickled into the river. The eel had remained below the rookery for several days, hiding underwater in the dark holes and passages of the tree roots, growing fat on fallen worms, leatherjackets and snails which the male birds dropped in the excitement of desire as they trod their wives. Over the seasons the eel had grown cunning, reaching a length of two feet and three inches which was too great for the comfort of a heron. His size exceeded the ambitions of the hunting mink and his sole fear was a single dog otter which had a track along the water's edge; the otter passed that way at night, a secret being, unnoticed by all except Pengelly and the keeper who recognised his seal on sloping banks of mud and sand. The eel carried a rusty hook in his gullet, evidence of a brief encounter with an astonished schoolboy before the eel had squirmed beneath the tree where the nylon was broken on a twisted root. On the moor at night frost gripped the peat sponge and froze the surface water into crusts of ice, the tributaries slowed causing the river to fall and clear. Spring was set aback.

For several hours after the wind swung to North East Setra remained in front of the fish trap wall, he felt the changed conditions and the chill of the new water made him lethargic; he would not run against the cold. Between dusk and dawn the water level dropped nine inches, the reduced depth over his back made him uneasy and he swam forward to a deep gulley where salmon rested, and there took up station in a group protected by a near vertical wall of rock on one side. For fifteen days the wind stayed between north and east and then swung to the west, but no rain fell in April. During the dry days the fish of the pool were motionless, hour after hour, stirring themselves from lethargy solely at dawn and dusk to jump to the diamond stars. At times they were harried by salmon fishers but the excitement of the high water had left them and none stirred to take a bait. White patches developed on the noses of three of their number and quickly spread in blotches on the salmon's backs. Setra took no notice of the fish which had the disease, did not avoid them or move away, but the infected members lost vitality and swam to the slack calm edges of the river where they waited in shallow water. Others with the disease from higher up the valley passed by, washed downstream, swept along by the current, unable to hold themselves against the flow in their weakened state. In time the river rolled them over, their silver bodies not yet dulled, but blotched with brown and white, sank, decayed and broke up on the river bed. The skulls, back-bones and greying skins were the last to rot away. The first cuckoo called in the valley at the end of April and swallows hawked early season flies which danced above the water. Trout rose, dimpling the surface of the calmer places and primroses bloomed, their yellow flowers in brave clusters promising warmer days to the wild daffodils of the river bank which nodded and swayed in agreement. Down the valley Craak fished silently below the trees. Food was hard to find for his greedy brood, young rabbits were scarce, the trout thin after the winter and froglets still of little size. Next month in May it would be different, fledgling birds, still struggling for flight, would be shaken down the long throat into his ample crop.

On May Day cloud coverage increased, blotting out the sun and sky; swallows and martins no longer hawked insects above the moorland tors but sped over the meadows of the valley. In the evening the rain started, small misty drops, then heavier splashes wet the dust of the pony tracks. Each splash joined the next and these tiny pools enlarged and ran downhill with other trickles to form streamlets. Dust at first floated on the surface but was drowned to join the crumbling peat which stained the water. Parched grasses sucked up moisture and swelled, growing to sustain the milk of grazing mares. Streams filled and brooks bubbled, white froth gathered under the banks and Setra felt the coming of the spate off the moors as he waited in Monk's Pool. For the whole day he had been restless, opening his mouth to taste the water, smelling the flow, swimming up to the neck of the pool to test the depth but each time he dropped back, being unable to press upstream through the shallow water over the pebbles and boulders of the stickle beyond. The raised temperature of the water excited him and one of the salmon jumped, crashing back in spray to the alarm of a dipper on a rock.

The rain reached the lower river after dark and continued throughout the night. At dawn worried hungry rooks fluttered over their nests, undecided whether to search the fields for food and leave their growing ugly youngsters to the cold and wet of rain, or brood on in hunger. Two days later a number of the nestlings died and were discarded to the river below where they were eaten by the eel. The water at first discoloured and then a brown stain spread down the valley of the lower river followed by a growing torrent which submerged the rocks, covered the footprints of fattening steers at the sandy cattle drinks, and carried away much flotsam. Simon the keeper walked the bank in satisfaction although unable to see into the brown flood. The spate would flush the valley, carry away the bodies of salmon putrefying on the river bed, bring a cleanliness, and fresh fish would come up from the sea. A drowned sheep floated by, legs in air, swirled on by the river. Simon walked back to his car and drove to the next weir up the river to watch for running fish. No need to worry now about a poacher creeping up the bank to cast a weighted treble hook across the salmon's backs for the fish were running and none remained stationary in the torrent. At the weir it would be different. There they had to leap, exposing themselves for a few seconds to the snatch of a gaff: there was a ready market at the back doors of Plymouth and Exeter. He drove five miles up the valley to Brock Weir, a smooth section of the river before it rose steeply in dashing falls and runs to the moor. A leat, blocked at the mouth by boards of oak, took water from above the weir into a channel to drive the wheel of a mill. With the coming of the flood Setra passed out of Monk's Pool and no one saw his going. He followed the tail of a heavy salmon which took advantage of the edges of the current, avoiding the rush of the centre of the river. On entering a new pool this salmon made a single leap before continuing the upstream run. Their migration was at a walking pace, steady, hugging the river bed, a purposeful progression. An inland town held them up for half a day, nauseated by the outflow of polluted water gushing from a pipe below the sewage farm. Setra took the lead, keeping to the far bank. He passed the pipe, travelled on between tree lined banks and swam strongly up the centre arch of a stone bridge, resting momentarily in front of one of the pillars. Buttressed from behind he paused, then passed on through a deep gulley followed by two smaller peal of three and four pounds.

In the fading light of the evening of 2 May the three swam up a mile of gentle water to enter the scoured out sanctuary of Brock Weir Pool. Setra rolled, revealing the broadness of his tail to Simon who watched from his seat on the oak beam which held an iron wheel with wormed shaft to raise the leat boards. Setra's chest now bore a raw patch the size of a pebble and the base of his tail was pink—abrasions caused by the roughness of the river bed. During the morning the rain had ceased on the moor, the bulge of water passing down the valley passed its peak and by nightfall the flow slowed, cleared and dropped.

At dawn Setra lay with his two companions where sand and gravel shallowed out at the pool tail. A salmon rested in front of them, opening and closing his mouth in irritation at the working of brown gill maggots. Setra had no maggots and the sea lice had dropped off, leaving him without external parasites. His colour had tarnished to a dull silver speckled with dark spots, the broad straight edge of his tail was dark and parchment thin. He had no desire to feed.

The warmth of late spring spread into the water and through the woods on either side, the buds of ash trees swelled and the white and pink candles of horse chestnuts fed the humming insects. Grannom flies hatched at noon to dance upon the lifting air, their grey bodies, lace wings and green egg sacs an invitation to passing swallows who sped above the water beneath the arch of overhanging boughs. Bluedart the kingfisher sat on a branch above the river, jerking his head up and down as he focused on the fry of brown trout outlined as transparent shadows shifting on the golden sand of the leat bed. Bluedart dived to reappear with an inch-long fish. He slapped the troutlet on the branch, whereupon its struggles ceased, enabling the kingfisher to swallow the fishlet. He had a nest in the upturned bole of a beech tree which had been blown over in a gale—the kingfisher had excavated the tunnel into the earth held in the roots; at the end of the hole was a clutch of three white eggs which his mate would increase before she started to sit. He arrowed away, uttering a piping call as a magpie fluttered over him.

In his cottage on the Tors moor Pengelly waited for me to collect him. We had agreed to fish the evening hours as

the spate receded and salmon settled in new lies. Pengelly
had slept little in the night, excited at the passing of the
rain which ceased to drum on the slate roof and rattle
against the windows. He had risen at first light to inspect
the Stoney Cross pool through binoculars—not that there
would be a fish there so early in the season, but he could
tell by the visibility of rocks and tufts of grass at water level
whether the river had dropped away. Having decided that
it would be too high in the morning lower down the river
he had telephoned me suggesting a visit to Brock Weir
after tea, taking a supper with us. Looking forward to this
he made a breakfast of toast, honey and coffee whilst
glancing out of the window at gaps in the clouds which
scudded over the moor. He took a stick and walked to
Rowan Tree gate to look down at Stoney Cross Pool—just
to make sure. The air parted with a ripping sound above
his head as a lapwing protested at his presence near her
nest. The lapwing plunged and twisted, uttering warning
cries before landing one hundred yards away where it
pretended to feed until Pengelly had left the area; the nest,
a bare scrape in the heather, held four pointed eggs of
green and streaky black. When the eggs hatched the fluffy
chicks would dry and run at once. He knew all about the
plover, the nest and the coming young—his worry in a few
days would be to avoid treading on the chicks. When
Pengelly walked back to the cottage the plovers took off to
mob a carrion crow, an egg thief and baby snatcher, which
passed over their territory. They bemused the crow which
became discomforted by the twists, turns, swoops and cries
of the plovers and retreated to a lone pine above the river.
Later he flew down to suck an egg in a duck's nest which
had been swamped in the flood. Triumphantly the lapwings

wheeled in the sky: "pee-wit, pee-wit, pee-wee" came the lonely cry as their wings zipped, rustled and cut the morning air.

On the way to the river in my car it was agreed that I would fish down to Brock Weir whilst Pengelly worked up a couple of hundred yards to the Weir pool, we would then eat our sandwiches at the end of the leat, sitting on the wooden foot bridge with our backs to the oak boards and feet dangling over the narrow channel.

I tied on an orange fly, a tube in which I have faith, and started to fish. All thoughts left me other than the passage of the fly and the jerking movements which I imparted. It swept in a curve across the river, traversed rough passages and searched the bays and pools. It was satisfying to roll out the line and use the rod to full advantage. In front of Pine Tree Island I had a touch, slight as a sunken leaf brushing the fly. I was sure a fish was there. A moment passed before the water erupted as he jumped, all the silver length and beauty of him shattered the surface. The rolling waves spread out, reduced, smoothed and settled. I tried him again. This time he took. In a curving, breath-taking, rolling surge he gathered the fly and took it down. I raised the butt when he had gone, the line straightened and the rod tip curved over to settle into a straining arc. "Steady on" I muttered, moving along the bank to a position opposite him "no hysterics, you don't want leaps and acrobatics. Keep up a steady draw to take some of the steam out of him". We stayed thus, me above with a well curved rod and him below, out of sight, static and mysterious. After five minutes I lowered my rod to set him off balance—he responded with a fast run to the other side, upstream of my stand. Just the ticket, I thought, if he keeps this up for a

little longer and I pile on the pressure he'll come back downstream and he'll be mine. In a while he tired and I was able to work him down to a quiet bay where I waded out with the net. He set himself to swim downstream, to pass me by, but I intercepted him and scooped him out.

Pengelly, waiting at Brock Weir, was full of congratulations. Having caught so many fish himself over the years there was no reason for jealousy on his part. "What a beauty, clean and fresh run, look at the sea lice, must have run the ten miles from Tormouth on this single flood. I'd put him at thirteen pounds—a truly lovely fish". We sat on the oak plank of the leat to share a dram from my flask, he using the silver cup whilst I tipped the glass neck between my teeth. Eating our sandwiches in silence he pulled the ring off a tin of beer, took two or three mouthfuls, waved his hand at the far bank where the weir spilled over to continue down the river and commented matter-of-factly "There's a fish over there, a small one, probably an early peal. I've risen him". He took a bite from an apple and another from a knob of cheese, chewing them in satisfaction. He rose, patted his tummy and with a grin said "Well, my turn upstream but first I'll just put that peal in the car". He cut off the orange salmon fly with a pair of scissors he carried on a string around his neck, selected a smaller silver and black fly which he tied on with knobbly arthritic fingers. Knots were becoming a problem, but not the casting, for the rod placed the fly just where he wished. On the third throw the fish came up in a fast curve—a supple agile sea trout. Twice more he rose the peal then, hanging the fly over the lie and drawing it away towards the far bank by a mend in the line, the peal took. The sea trout ran for the foam below the weir, jumped twice in the turmoil then shot off downstream out of the pool. Pengelly followed as best he could, stumbling over rocks, passing the top of the arched rod over bushes until he was able to beach the peal in a sandy bay. Panting, he admitted "Not so young these days. Time was when I would have skipped down here before the fish, to await his arrival." We carried the peal back to join the salmon in the boot of the car before I set off down the river. Pengelly rested on the oak plank "I've had enough. All I can manage these days".

In the weir pool Setra waited. He saw one of his companions behave in a strange way, and for a while he had followed the hooked peal in its fight. When the water quietened he returned to an idle torpor, flanked on one side by the three pound peal; the place of the four pound sea trout was filled by a brown trout whose gold body blended with the colour of the sand. Below the water surface above the weir an early mayfly nymph struggled up towards the light. The nymph twisted in the clinging water film and the turmoil of this action split the body shuck, releasing the dun which dried its wings and tail whisks in the warmth of the evening air. With feet dimpling the surface the dun was swept over the weir and down the pool. From the river bed little could be seen of the insect other than the pinpricks of its legs on the water skin. Setra watched. As a juvenile parr he had fed on mayflies and an instinct made him rise and take the fly. Pengelly saw and remembered it all: the nose, the sucking mouth, the curve of the back and then the tail, wide, straight-edged and strong.

Four weeks went by, spring changed to early summer, but the days were dry and the river shrank. In the weir pool Setra waited in the shallowing river, he felt stale and lethargic as the water warmed. In early June he hid below the weir gap, concealed from passing walkers and a poaching man who searched the holding pools by day, peering into the depths through Polaroid spectacles. At night he felt relief from the rays of the sun and shifted out to the smooth flow of the run-off to lie with others beneath the stars.

CHAPTER 4

Harvest Peal by Moonlight

IN MID-JUNE Pengelly climbed the wooden ladder to the barn loft slowly and with care. At the top he paused to wipe the sweat from his brow and upper lip; it was sultry and a storm seemed likely. The gloom in the loft dispersed slowly as his eyes became accustomed to the windowless interior, and he heard the owlets before being able to make them out. Hisses and clicking mandibles revealed the youngsters who studied the intruder with wide hostile eyes, snapped their beaks in fear and leaned back as he picked up one of the four. He examined the fluffy bundle which seemed all wool, little weight and the head a size too large for the body. The flight feathers were apparent and hardening, in another week they'd be on the roof and sitting on the tack room door. Whiteface watched from the ridge of the building, flew in mock attack at Pengelly and then drifted away over the moor to hunt. The owl had become accustomed to the old man's visits for he, and his ancestors, had known him over many breeding seasons.

He climbed down the ladder, crossed the yard to the cottage, took a tin of beer from the cupboard, poured it into a pewter tankard and sat on the bench by the open window. Swallows and house martins hawked insects over the heather whilst bands of swifts chased each other around the buildings; they then screamed away across the moor before climbing into the sky. Turning, speeding and twisting the swifts returned to dash straight into their nest cracks in the stone walls of the barn.

Clouds thickened over the cottage in the afternoon, the sky took on an orange tinge, thunder cracked over the western slopes and lightning cut the sky. The old man waited hopefully on the bench until the first warm solid splashes hit the grey dust of the yard. It had been so long coming, many weeks of drought without the chance of a salmon and too early for peal fishing in the dark. He watched with satisfaction as Rowan Tree Gate was blotted out by curtains of rain. He raised himself to his feet and walked to the door to lean against the upright on one side and look into the yard. To savour the rain to the full he took a few steps forward, lifted his wrinkled face and felt the softness of the raindrops run down the channels in his skin, fall on his brow, his lips and tongue; even the air smelled fresh. This was a good wet, the river would rise and in would come groups of sea trout from the sea. They always started to arrive at the end of June, and continued to build their numbers in the river until the end of August and sometimes into September. It was a time Pengelly loved. The fields took on a golden hue before the combine harvesters cut the wheat and barley of the lowland farms—how long was it since he'd seen a field of oats? He also harvested, for a share of the bounty of the river was his by taking sea trout at night—harvest peal as the small summer fish were called. He looked forward during winter evenings to the summer sea trout nights, remembering the best of them, great events when he took a heavy peal under the stars or a salmon in the twilight. At such times it was good to be by oneself, to shake off the rattle of conversation, to walk unseen, to fish unnoticed by the wild creatures, to be absorbed and accepted by the night. Pengelly knew his good fortune to live in such a place: to be touched by the free wind, to stretch his eyes to the far horizons and the buzzards in the sky above the hills. He checked himself—it was all very well going on like this, but if he wanted to catch a peal tomorrow night, if the rain ceased and a small spate came and passed, he'd better have some sleep after supper. He went inside to make a meal by slicing the white meat from the breast of a cold cooked chicken which his daughter had brought to the cottage. Outside he cut a lettuce from the vegetable patch, the large green leaves were splashed with grit thrown up by the raindrops—it was all very satisfactory, for the lettuces would freshen and the radish seeds he had sown would germinate. Lettuce, cold chicken, a pickled onion and a slice of wholemeal bread—who would wish for more, and there would be just one plate with knife and fork to wash up when he finished. The knife was sharp he noticed with satisfaction: he couldn't stand blunt knives. He chewed in a thoughtful absent-minded way because there was a decision to make, a balanced choice. Tomorrow he could either spend the day at home, reserving his strength for a night at the peal, or he could have a crack at the salmon in the morning, and perhaps the afternoon as well. At one time, a few years back, he might have managed both day and night, but now he no longer had the stamina. As he looked back over the season, so far as it had progressed, he was troubled by the dryness of the year and of other recent years. He searched the recesses of his memory for facts, then rising crossed to his desk for his fishing diary and turned the pages to the summary at the end of each year. Yes, there it was, the last good wet summer was five years ago—he'd had seventeen salmon on the fly, of which six came in August when it had rained so much that he restricted his catch. Years ago there came a time in a wet summer when he couldn't give any more fish away, and couldn't stand the sight of another plateful, however good the mayonnaise. He never sold a fish. It didn't seem right to sell them, converting their individual lives into anonymous five pound notes. He hadn't sold a salmon since the year his daughter was born and he was really up against it—must be fifty years since he caught that fish. He pondered: how the time had flown, and here he was, a worn out husk of his former self. There was so much to remember, a treasure house in his head from which he was able to extract long past events one at a time for examination. The thought of this was a comfort; he hadn't looked back in that way many times before, having always tried to look ahead. Now, after long and hopeful anticipation of a day on the river, he never quite managed to do what was planned. It must be that he moved more slowly, for certainly the days did not grow shorter. Well, he had these memories and when he grew tired, and felt it too great an effort to fish so frequently, he could fill the gaps between with thoughts drawn from the library of his life.

The beer had made him sleepy but he brushed his wandering memories aside. Where was he—oh yes, whether to fish for salmon tomorrow or sea trout tomorrow night. It would be best to go for the peal, for the night fishing months were fewer than those of the longer salmon season. The decision made, he pondered where to go. It would be too early yet for Stoney Cross—they rarely reached the higher moor in any numbers before August, except for a few large ones, and they were the devil's own job to catch. That large fish he'd seen, the one with the great tail, where would he go on this spate? Certainly he wouldn't be in Brock Weir, he'd leave that pool tonight when the river rose, and maybe run three or four miles, or even further, for the season was getting on. He could be in Stoney Cross, but it was unlikely he would reach that pool, and the chances of coming up with him were remote—it would be better to go for the first of the harvest peal and be sure of one or two, and if there happened to be a good fish, well, that would be a bonus. So which pool? Back to Monk's, that was it, retrace the steps of the early season for these later running peal. They were bound to be there—perhaps it would be as well to have a look during daylight just to make sure.

Pengelly telephoned me—would I drive him to Monk's Pool tomorrow afternoon to assess the peal population? If we went about six o'clock we could make a survey with polaroids, confirm the usual positions of the shoals and then have a bite at the Poundsworthy Inn before returning to the river for a couple of hours fishing in the dark. He sounded excited at the prospect of the first night of the season, a walk along the bank, the meal at the pub and a chance to exchange ideas and information. The arrangement made, the old man went to bed. The wooden treads of the stairs creaked at each step and a board on the landing sprung under his weight. He sometimes thought of taking up the carpet to nail down the plank, but it didn't seem important. He put on his pyjamas and lay on his back under the sheet and a single blanket, held his breath momentarily and listened to the sounds beyond the open window. The rain was easing off, which would give the river a chance to clear before the following night. A tawny owl called from the copse at the bottom of the track which led to the road, and he heard a plover's cry. Some birds were diurnal. Sometimes he wondered about the heron—did he feed at night? It didn't seem possible that the bird could see to strike with his beak, particularly into the water, but they sometimes arrived at the river at dusk. Now why would they do that if not to hunt? In a while he fell asleep on his back whilst still listening through the open window and considering the puzzle of the heron.

The next afternoon I put my things together. The 9 ft fly rod and the reel with the white floating line. White was so much easier to see on the water at night and I couldn't be bothered with a line which sank. When the fish ceased surface activity I usually went home and there was little doubt Pengelly would be pleased to do the same. Waders, net, priest and torch, and the bag with the flies, the nylon and the bits and pieces which every fisherman collects.

At the river we wandered along the bank in the evening sunshine. Pengelly was always ahead, a little puffed for breath but full of enthusiasm as he climbed a few feet up a tree to look down into the water. At the tail of Monk's Pool the river shallowed out on our side but was deep under the far bank. It was a beautiful place, full of promise for the night, and as I watched from the bank a silver flank flickered momentarily—a fresh run peal. I lay on the grass with my chin in my hands to watch Pengelly climb a tree stump for a better view. In time I discerned the fish. The darkness of the river below my bank slowly yielded its secrets and the grey torpedo shapes of sea trout developed: large sea trout of two and three pounds. The straight edges of the tails were the first giveaway and their mouths, which sometimes gaped to reveal a momentary whiteness, fixed their positions.

The old man descended from the stump which grew a covering screen of leaves through which he had peered, and crept, doubled up, along the bank, shielded by a waterside line of white cow parsley flowers. He lay down beside me. "There's a shoal of about eight, fifteen yards below you on this side, almost under the stump, none of 'em large. There's another group strung out towards the run-off on the other side; most of them about twelve ounces or a pound. In front of that submerged rock in the middle there's a good fish of about four pounds and another of the same size a yard or two above him". We digested the matter for a while, each wondering who would fish the pool tail. "Look here," he offered "you gave me first crack when I took that salmon in March. It's your turn now, and anyway I'm just as happy to listen and watch. I'll have a cast or two later, or go upstream below the rookery".

We retraced our steps and drove to the Poundsworthy Inn. I cracked my head on the oak lintel over the doorway as I entered the bar. "Built for diddy men," observed Pengelly. "They were all the same, the locals, down here a couple of hundred years ago, short they were. If you'd gone to bed in a pub on the moor in the nineteen twenties the chances were your feet would hang over the end—particularly a long heron like you. That's because the beds would have been fifty years old, hair mattresses on them too. In the old queen's time, Victoria I mean, the food was neither balanced nor plentiful; there was little heat in the granite farmsteads and the children grew short, wiry and tough. Mean too. They had to be mean, there was nothing to spare for frivolity. They're still close with the cash today, but that's an inherited trait".

We ate our pork pies with mustard, and followed them with a slice from a cottage loaf and a hunk of cheese. I was on my second pint when the old man looked at me: "Shouldn't have any more of that if I were you—it's cold standing in the river and you don't want to wade out to pump ship, disturbs the fish".

On the bank at Monk's Pool we watched the light fade until the white flowers of the cow parsley blended into the brambles on the far bank. The final carrion crows had flown silently up the valley above the water to roost in the branches of a Scots pine, and we had seen three bats flit by. I whispered "In Ireland they always wait until they have seen three. Two are not enough and to start as early as that will frighten the sea trout".

"How does an Irishman tell one from from another?" asked Pengelly in a pithy question. "He may just have seen one early one three times".

"By the size I suppose"

"Sounds crazy," he observed, settling himself comfortably on the bank for a nap whilst I set about the peal. The light had almost gone as I picked up my rod and took hold of the fly which was soaking in a little pool with the nylon leader. A peal jumped under the far bank and then another, a good fish this one of two or three pounds which split the surface and crashed back. Smaller peal leaped as well, shimmering and vibrating in their silver skins as they sprang towards the stars.

"The moon'll be up soon and when it shines upstream it'll dazzle you. Best get on with it. Won't grow any darker now". Pengelly was sitting up, full of expectation and enthusiasm.

I slid quietly down the bank into the water, muddying the seat of my trousers. I moved forward until the current swept about my knees, working my way out to within casting distance of the far bank. At my waist was the net with the white painted rim which would show up in the dark, and a trout bass to hold the peal. Around my neck a cord reached down to the metal priest in my pocket.

Drawing line from the reel I started to false cast in the air, separating the forward and backward throws to avoid tangles, then let the line shoot forward to fall lightly on the water. The fly pitched in beyond the line, the tiny ring it made on the black surface of the water illuminated by the glow of the eastern sky where the moon was rising. As the current swept the line it bellied in a curve which pulled the fly around until it hung below me. Next time there was a slight nip from a peal or a wild brown trout as the fly covered a further foot of water. I cast again and retrieved the line over my right forefinger a few inches at a time, the draw of my pull directly in touch with the fly, the rod almost horizontal, my eyes searching and fingers feeling for information. An awareness comes to me when a peal takes gently—for a moment it is as though an obstruction has been touched.

When the line stops swinging, my brain registers the reason and the peal reacts after a second in a flurry of splashes as fear takes hold. That first pull is transformed at once into an electric connection between us, all becomes speed, spray, fighting rod and desperate fish. I hung on hard to this one which ran upstream at once, passed me, on and on for fifteen yards into the deepness of the pool, and then he made two frightening leaps. He was gone. I stripped in line as fast as the left arm would pull. No, he'd just run back fast and was a rod's length off my legs, heading for the far bank. He churned, then pulled steadily for the bushes on the other side, reached the black deeps below the white blur of the cow parsley flowers and then I drew him away. The rod was now high, well arched, I could tell he was close, and then a white bar, his flank, became visible on the dark water and the net scooped him out. I knocked him on the head with the priest whilst still in the net, felt for the fly in the upper jaw, and avoiding the sharpness of the teeth released the hook and dropped the fish into the bass hanging on my belt.

"Well done. What size?"

"About two and a half pounds," I replied, and settled down to continue at the pool. After a while another joined the first, but when I called out to Pengelly there was no reply.

The old man stood on a gravel bar just below the head of the rookery pool. With care he adjusted his position, placing himself with a tree blotting out the brilliance of the moon. He liked to fish by moonlight to see what he was doing, but he didn't like the moonbeams in his face. He started, casting upstream whilst retrieving faster than the current washed the fly downstream. He was confident in his position, the sand bar suited him for he couldn't slip and it was an easy matter to beach a fish without the complication of a net. The only thing he had to watch was not to put down his wet reel, for the grit would stick on the drum and grate in the action. He cast to an illuminated patch of water to see the fly plop out and satisfy himself he hadn't any tangles. He could almost tell if the fly had tangled on the nylon by the sound of the casting in the air, but it was as well to make certain. He moved two paces down the bar after a few casts and there took a small sea trout of about a pound, sliding the fish up onto the gravel after a brief fight. Taking out the hook he tapped the fish on the head and threw it over his shoulder onto the grass. At that moment a larger sea trout leaped under the trees to bash down and create waves. Pengelly muttered "All right m'dear. Plenty of time". He shuffled along the gravel bar without vibration or noise and, as he came closer, dropped to his knees to cut his silhouette against the sky. These were the times he loved, when there was a good fish to be taken and it was one against the other—an old man's experience with gentle practised hands seeking to break the barrier of caution which surrounded an old peal wise in the migration perils. He put four casts over the place without response. The water was flat. Nothing moved. He was neither surprised nor discouraged. He turned his back on the river and still on his knees bit off the fly and threaded on a Silver Stoat's Tail tube. The moon helped with light, and the sensitivity of his feeling tongue assisted his fingers with the knot. On the fifth cast he whispered to himself "Come on. Please God let him come, and if he does I'll remember to thank you, though I might not remember all at once". And the peal took and fought Pengelly in the dark until his wrist ached and he was forced to support the rod with two hands. "Don't let him go God—perhaps I don't deserve him, but don't let him go". Isolated in time and darkness they struggled until the fish was guided into a shallow pool and beached. Pengelly thumped him on the head with a stone and then sat down to recover. I found him sitting on the grass admiring his catch. "I've had two" he said "Do you know, there was a slug chewing at the small one which I caught first—bloody things. Can't stand slugs. Only thing to do is put the fish in a plastic bag".

We crossed the meadow to the car, our boots lifeless on tired legs, and looked forward to a whisky at the cottage. An owl hooted above the river and if Pengelly hadn't been there I would have swept the trees with my torch in a spasm of fear. Crossing the moor a fox, caught in the headlights, trotted off the road and rabbits hopped on the grass verge. A badger trundled up the lane to the cottage, broke into a gallop as the car came closer, then slid under a gate.

I left him after the whisky—he was heating a kettle to make a hot water bottle "my bones grow stiff and tired these days".

Pengelly heard the sound of the car fade; he picked up the wet fish bass, took out his two peal and laid them on the kitchen draining board. The weighing scale showed the larger one to be four pounds and one ounce, and the smaller fish was just under one pound. He put them back on the board and pressed their flesh with his thumb—both were as firm as he would expect when caught so close to the sea: they would eat well. He considered their passage up the river, knowing that they would reach the Stone Cross pool in August, by which time they would have darkened in colour and softened in texture. Monk's Pool was the place to take a good eating peal, but by September, the end of the month anyway, they had all passed through and the only way to come up with them was on the moor. He poured himself another tot of whisky and climbed the creaking stairs in satisfaction, pulled off his trousers and shirt and collapsed into bed, clutching the hot water bottle to his chest. He was growing too old for these capers, he realized, for stumbling about in the dark. Well, he'd made up his mind to wear out, not rust out, and to live fully to the last.

On the morning of 17 June Setra moved out of Brock Weir Pool, leaping into the torrent of water which gushed through the weir gap and forcing his way upstream on the rising flood. For five miles he followed the river trail with others of his tribe until he reached the margins of the moor, the broken rocky places where the river narrowed and flowed with life and speed. There he waited and rested in the dark place known as Rock Hole, lying under the bank beneath an overhanging clump of heather to one side of the main surge of the current. After dark, in clearing, falling water he swam on again to take advantage of the last of the spate. As the moon dipped below the horizon, and Pengelly went to bed half a day's walk up the valley he entered Fox pond, a wide sandy bottomed splay of water where wild creatures drank at night and the wading cattle swished the flies away by day.

CHAPTER 5

The Encounter with the Great Sea Trout

F OR FIVE WEEKS Setra remained in Fox Pond. There was no spawning urgency within him, the milt sacs in his body cavity remained small and the month clock in his head did not yet force him on to the spawning beds; this urgency would come with the winter. It was a time of waiting, the weeks continued dry and the river shrank to the lowest level of the year. By day he hid in the deepest coolest water in the shadow of an underwater boulder, his head tucked below an overhanging ledge, whilst his tail, almost immobile, protruded from beneath the stone. At dusk he played briefly with other peal and the salmon who were also on their spawning run—play which took him arrowing below the water skin which stretched and lifted over his back as he chased others or was followed across the pool. Sometimes he leaped, not knowing why. Darkness brought freedom of movement; a little coolness came to him, born down the valley by the running water which had been stroked over the stickles by the chill night breeze. With this freshness came a resurgence of vitality. Some nights he lay with others at the shallow tail of the pool, just above the final stones where the water was sucked downstream. Many peal lay in this run-off after dark—the only sign to a watcher on the bank being

41

the vertical leap of the smaller fish when youth forced them to release their pent-up energy. With the dawn, when light brought colour to the flowers, the sea trout played again before retiring to the shadows and the deeps.

By the sixth week Setra had become accustomed to the wild birds and animals which visited the pool; he was no longer fearful of the mallard duck whose brood of seven swam beneath the overhanging bank. She had nested five feet above the river bank in March in the hollow ivy-covered top of a rotted tree stump. The tree had snapped off some years previously in a gale, having died under the grip of the ivy. The body of the tree was swept away by the river which rolled it wildly downstream whilst twisted clutching branches broke the surface for a last grasp at the sky. The duck had flown up to the top of the stump to pick out the rotten scraps of wood. She had made a bowl in the centre, lined it with leaves, grass and down from her breast and there she laid fourteen light green eggs. For four weeks she incubated the clutch, hidden by the screen of ivy leaves which grew over the edges of the bowl. She blended with the shades of the rotten wood and sat, still and silent, until the eggshells cracked. Of the fourteen eggs, twelve had hatched, releasing tiny balls of fluff. The ducklings remained in the nest for a day under the wings and breast of the mallard until they dried. She then fluttered to the water, calling her brood with soft persuasive quacks; the tinies followed her, bouncing off the trunk to plop on to the water or fall on the bank of grass and stones. Two infertile eggs left behind grew cold—they were spied by a carrion crow which pierced the shells with its beak, broke them open and feasted. Woodlice emerged at night to absorb the final nourishment, and the pieces of shell sank out of sight in the debris at the flattened bottom of the nest. In early July the brood was reduced to six by hunting mink, and a magpie which few away with a duckling in its beak. The duck did not notice the loss of two who fell down a hole from which they were unable to climb. She now led her family under the river banks where they dibbled for caddis larvae in gritty cases, ate the tadpoles of the moorland frogs, and plucked at insects on the stems of river plants. When the young duck flew Setra was frightened by their splashings, but he became used to their silhouettes against the sky and no longer swam to hide.

On the fourth night of the sixth week of the drought the clear cut sickle of a new moon joined the stars. Together they lifted darkness from the earth, the water became blacker than the land and a man could see to fish. Setra drifted down to the run-off at dusk; there he watched the sickle through the ripples in which it danced and flirted with the stars.

By the seventh day of August Pengelly felt that the peak of summer had passed. One moment it was June: birds sang freely, swifts nested in the crevices of the barn and golden days lay ahead. In August the swifts departed, and breeding activities of wild creatures declined and the days shortened. On the river he had seen broods of young duck which could fly, and in his walks upon the moor he noticed the changing colour of the heather which flowered into a purple carpet highlighted by white tufts of bog cotton. The trees were changed—gone was the softness of light green leaves which now took on a harder shade, and green unripe berries formed on the rowan tree. It had also been raining for a week.

The river rose rapidly as rain ran off the dried up land into the watercourse. The bed was washed of algae and for a while the water became thick, acid and brown. The old man walked the banks in gumboots on the seventh morning, easing himself over the rougher places with a thumb stick of ash which he had cut out of the overgrown hedge bordering the lane to his cottage. The river was running a foot above the July level and he saw many salmon head and tail in the brown froth-edged water as they made their way upstream. The fish had left their usual lies: they were spread out over gravel banks which were too shallow in the drought, beside the necks of pools, close to reeds and in other shallow places. He saw small salmon of four and five pounds in weight, silver in colour, athletic in streamlined shape, which had run up from the sea to the high moor on the flood of seven days. These were grilse, the first arrivals of the invading shoals of one sea-winter salmon which would build their numbers in the river throughout August and September. Latecomers would follow to jump through the sea pool ladder in October and hurry on to catch the leaders of their race. He recalled a year in which there had been a five-month drought; broken by the mid-September equinoctial gales which brought torrential rain. He had sat beside Brock Weir one afternoon until the light went, watching the grilse jump the obstruction at the rate of one a minute. He was reassured of the survival of their race as he saw each fish nose out the position of the gap, swing around, drop back, accelerate and leap wide-eyed through the opening to disappear into the smoother waters above the weir. He admired these fish which survived the perils of the ocean and now returned to the rivers of their birth and the spawning grounds close to his cottage. After being spawned they had matured step by step in a two-year river growth, moving downstream gradually as newly hatched alevins complete with a sustaining yolk sac, transparent hiding fry, and darting parr with fingers marks upon their flanks. Finally, as silver smolts eight inches long, they left the fresh water in March and April for the sea and now returned after sixteen or more months of rich feeding in the North Atlantic ocean. They were of the river family, natives of the moor, and Pengelly welcomed them; he had also seen small peal at the end of that drought when the flooded river overflowed the length of Brock Weir. These little ones swam almost vertically up the sheet of water curving over the wide obstruction, their tails moving faster than his eye could follow, their bodies vibrating in determination. He walked on, tripped over a stone, jerked upright and brought himself back to the present. He daydreamed and harked back more these days. "Never see it all again," he thought, and neither would anyone else, for the world had changed, pressures on the wild things were increasing and even fishermen no longer had the time to stand, to wonder and to stare. He took a few steps to the river edge, walked in to the water until it reached almost to the top of his rubber boots and then looked down at his feet—he could see them clearly through the whisky-coloured flow. He paused: if he could see his boots a salmon would be able to see his fly, and although little clumps of green grass, which were normally above the surface, were still submerged it was obvious that the level was falling. On the bank was a line of stranded flotsam: the dried stems of rushes, twigs, leaves and an empty bottle. This line was now six inches above the water. His eyes sharpened, dreams fled, and he set off along the edge of Stoney Cross pool to eat his lunch and prepare for salmon fishing in the afternoon.

At the cottage he ate absent-mindedly, seated at the kitchen table by the open door leading to the yard. He decided to start in the stickles above Stone Cross, give them a good going over, work through the pool itself from both banks and finish up at the pots below. You never knew the result of a cast or two into each pot—the small shallow rocky places only held running fish in high water, and the salmon could be of any size from grilse to those of fifteen or twenty pounds. By August fish of all sizes had reached the moor and their numbers would continue to increase throughout the autumn. He could remember one day, years ago, when he had lost a fish from the pots—his steel hook breaking at the bend. Since then he called the hole Broken Hook Pot. One forgot the fish which were landed, most of them anyway, but a lost salmon was engraved upon the memory. He rarely lost a fish these days through playing them incorrectly, a hook bending out or the leader breaking. Of course, some came unhooked, but that was bound to happen. For a while he mused to himself, then pushed his plate to one side, folded his arms upon the wooden table and fell asleep, his tufty-edged bald head resting on his forearms.

Outside in the yard and around the buildings house martins gathered flies from the air for their twittering offspring whose heads squeezed out of the openings of the mud cup nests beneath the cottage eaves. By the end of the month all would be fledged, feeding themselves, playing in groups in the air, and the nests would be abandoned to the sparrows until the following spring. The sparrows carried untidy wisps of hay into the cups and with their wings and feet broke the delicate restricted entrances of mud which the martins had glued into place with saliva.

The sparrows were noisy, argumentative, shallow-minded and inconsiderate of the fragile homes of the martins—when one nest was filled with rubbish until pieces of the cup fell away, rendering it uninhabitable, they occupied another.

Pengelly's mouth fell open and he snored. After a few minutes this noise awoke him. He looked through the door at the sky, rose stiffly, joint by joint, walked outside and felt the mild wind.

He took the spliced salmon rod from the pegs on the wall, ran the line through the rings and set up fly and leader. He pulled his socks over the bottoms of his trousers, pressed his legs down into his thigh boots and slung the salmon net on a leather strap over his back. He patted his pockets to feel that all was there: a tin of flies, a spool of nylon, the baler twine to carry a fish, chocolate and an apple. Closing the door he walked away to Rowan Tree Gate.

For his age he moved easily. He was eager, stirred by the prospect of searching out the newly arrived salmon which would be restless before they settled. They would continue to explore the pools for at least another day; gradually vacating the shallow tails as the water fell away, then moving forward to the centres and the throats for the cover provided by deep turbulent water. It was an exciting prospect. He was content and hugged his soul. He always felt like this before starting to fish, even as a small boy. Long ago when nine or ten years old he had been taken by his father in the summer holidays to an hotel with a lake in Shropshire. As he lay in bed before breakfast with the sun streaming in through the window, causing a glow in his closed eyes, he had felt the warmth of anticipation spread over him at the prospect of the totally enjoyable day ahead.

After breakfast his father and grandfather left their footprints on the dew-dropped grass as they took him to the lake where an ancient fisherman lived in the tarred roofed, wooden waterside hut on the far bank. His grandfather, a tall man with a great nose, cupped his hands to his mouth and called "John Cox" and again after a pause "John Cox". There would be a stirring on the other side as the door opened and a stooped figure emerged, stepped into a punt and rowed across to them. Craggy-whiskered and of few words, he took the boy Pengelly into his boat and rowed away to the hut, leaving his father and grandfather watching and growing smaller on the bank.

John Cox taught him to fish. For bait they used maggots from long dead pike which the waterman had strung up for the flies in a tree close to his hut. The pike hung by their tails with open mouths, twisting, twirling and swinging in the breeze, and the boy had held a can under each mouth as instructed, whereupon Cox tapped the dried body with a stick and maggots dropped into the can. They sat in the punt on the smooth expanse of water to watch a red cork float, below which a length of shotted gut disappeared into the depths where three or four maggots dangled on a hook. If they kept still in the boat the float would bob as a perch took the bait. If the red top dived below the surface the boy struck, and up would come a struggling perch to be swung into the boat and tapped upon the head. He ate those fish fried in breadcrumbs—golden crusty little fellows full of bones.

Forgetting his dreams and passing through the gate under the rowan tree he looked down on the turbulent river to see whether another angler fished the pools, but there was nobody, only sheep nibbling at the short grass. Crows flew across the sky, altering course to avoid him, and a buzzard circled in the wind.

He started on the top stickle, keeping back a pace or two from the water's edge, using the length of the rod which reached over the river, enabling him to remain out of sight of nearby fish. He cast the fly to the far side, switched upstream, and with the line drooping from the rod tip watched it swim back across the river. It was fulfilling: the pleasure of casting the fly where he wished and of speeding or slowing the retrieve. He did not see the salmon take his fly. The first indication was the altered angle of the floating line, the tip of which had been drawn down, then came a heavy stop, a solidness, followed by a pull which tightened the line and raised it from the water. His fingers resisted the pull and the hook went home into the salmon's jaw. Pengelly stumbled downstream over the uneven bank until he was opposite the fish. Rod arched high he looked for a sign which might reveal the size of the salmon, but as yet there was just the blackness of the river. He remained thus, taking energy out of the fish, and seven or eight minutes passed before the salmon, pulled off balance as he lowered the rod whilst changing the position of his aching arms, turned and swam fast out of the tail of the pool. Pengelly tried to stop him by releasing all pressure and stripping line from the reel, but the fish had power and the momentum of the river and would not be stopped. The old man let the reel run free and followed. He tripped over rocks, fell, scrambled through bushes, filled his waders as he entered the river to work around a bankside tree and, heart pounding, caught up one hundred yards down the stream. Gasping and trembling he arrived to see the salmon roll. He pulled the tag of the strap holding the net to his back and extended the shaft, lowered himself thigh deep into the water and coaxed the fish upstream of his stand. The first time he tried to swim the fish down head first into the net the salmon summoned reserves of energy, arrowing away to mid-stream below the old man's position. The line tightened dangerously as Pengelly lowered the rod butt against the inside of his thigh, and with this leverage worked the salmon back above him. This time he turned the fish closer to the bank and swam him down into the submerged net. He turned to the bank and pulling several yards of line from the reel flung the rod up onto the grass. He climbed up with the fish in the net, his thighs shook, gasps of air failed to satisfy his heaving chest, but he reached the safety of the flat earth where he hit the salmon on the head. He now lay down exhausted, but later raised his legs to allow the water to cascade from inside his waders onto the grass—this done he sat up and examined the fish. The salmon was a heavy red cock fish of about eighteen pounds; an ugly creature with a hooked white kype on the lower jaw which fitted into a socket of gristle under the nose. Not a pretty sight, but none the less a triumph, being the heaviest fish of the season. Pengelly passed the baler twine through the gills and out of the mouth, looped one end around the wrist of the tail and tied the ends together to make a handle. Raising himself from his knees he straightened his back with a grunt and flexed his aching shoulders. The tussle with the salmon had taken him so far down river that he now stood above Stoney Cross Pool beside the rough-hewn granite cross. He rested his rod against one of the stubby arms of stone and glanced up at the glassless eyes of the abandoned farmhouse standing against wind-blackened beech trees on the slope above the river. The final inhabitants must have stared out of those windows in despair at the deep pool where their child had drowned whilst playing on the peat banks. They erected the cross and left the moor thereafter. The house then commenced a slow decay.

He stared in reverie at the river curling under the far bank where the child had slipped, and as he did Setra nosed out at the neck of the pool, showing his back and then the broad square-ended tail which waved above the surface as he turned. "The great peal of Brock Weir?" the old man questioned. He was tired in his body and in his spirit after catching the salmon, but the sight could not be ignored. It was beyond him to say "I've had enough", to be defeated by age and his tired and trembling legs. Setra took the salmon fly on the fifth cast and swam under the bank where he was hidden by the bubbles at the pool entrance. In a while the old man's steady pressure on the line drew him out and he swirled below the surface. For a second Setra saw Pengelly outlined against the sky. The sea trout twisted, momentarily lost control of his tired body and floated belly up; he recovered and dashed for the deeps where he swam under a washed down sunken fence post. A moment or two went by before the old man realised he had been snagged. He pulled on the line, and then used a great force which stirred the slime-covered post on the river bed. The river swung the post to the side where Pengelly swore as he unwrapped the broken nylon from a rusty nail protruding from the wood.

Setra rested under the rock shelf. His tail waved behind the boulder and to his rear a length of nylon trailed in the current.

Pengelly climbed slowly up the hill to Rowan Tree Gate, his right shoulder sagged under the weight of the salmon, his left by the rod, and his mind by the loss of the sea trout.

51

At the garden gate he paused to catch his breath which came in short and shallow. He laid the salmon on the draining board of the kitchen sink and walked heavily to the dresser. The whisky revived him and he turned on the radio to catch the weather forecast before going into the yard to look down at the distant pool. Leaning against the door jamb a tight band of pain encircled his chest. Moving to the kitchen table he reached for the telephone and called his daughter who came at once, helped him upstairs, scolding all the time, and tucked him up in bed with an aspirin and a glass of whisky. Later, he went to live with her and she entrusted me with the key to the empty cottage.

CHAPTER 6

The Cycle of Life

SETRA REMAINED IN the pool of the Stone Cross for two months until the November winds swept the last of the leaves from the lichen-covered oaks of Gnarled Oak Wood. The oldest trees were few, for the wood had formed and then degenerated over many centuries. Those oaks which survived were crouched and deformed, supporting their trunks on roots which twined between the stones whilst leaning on weathered branches which rested on others of their kind and drooping, pressed upon the earth. Birch trees of soft and recent pulp grew thinly, lighting the wood with their whitened bark. The birches did not last; the malaise of the acid ground rotted them, the wind cut them down and they collapsed to be consumed by orange fungi, beetles and the rain let in by the woodpecker. The leaves of oak and birch mingled in the wind which blew them into the stream running through the valley of the wood. The water accepted them from the wind and bore them on. The leaves swept past Setra on their way to dissolution.

The appearance of the sea trout had changed. His flanks had darkened and assumed a reddish tinge, his vent protruded slightly and his tail was slit along the rays. He still rested beneath the ledge of stone from which he dropped back at times to rub his jaw on an edge of granite. White fungus covered one side of his head and the gill cover where he had rubbed at the hook of Pengelly's fly. The nylon still trailed behind his body where it waved in front of the nose of a smaller cock peal which had taken up station behind the ailing fish. Three yards in front of Setra the grey shadow of a hen of four pounds was discernible in the shadows. The belly of Sealass was swollen by three thousand eggs and her vent resembled the puckered sucker of a limpet plucked from a seaside rock. With the coming of the leaves Sealass grew restless to fulfil herself; she swam to the neck of the pool and with persistence found a way up to the flat waters. For a mile Setra followed her tail until they branched into the finger stream of the oak wood. Following the beds and curves of the stream, the narrow channels and the wider pebble beds, they passed many pairs of spawning salmon. Later Setra and Sealass settled in shallow water between the banks of Gnarled Oak Wood. A tree overhung his resting place and drips from the branches made rings on the surface of the constricted water. Setra took no notice of the drips or of a brightly coloured jay which landed in the tree, tilted its head to one side and watched the activity below. The jay was the sentry of the countryside. He challenged intruders with raucous cries, mobbed cats, stoats and the sleepy tawny owls whose wish was to be left in peace huddled against the ivy-covered trunks of trees. The jay peered down, chattered and called loudly, summoning two more of his tribe to add their cries of alarm at the sinuous dark creature running, stopping and then galloping along the bank of the stream. The mink stopped, rose on his back legs and chattered angrily at the jays whose scolding rose hysterically as they clamoured in the branches above his head. A magpie joined them, adding his clatter to the sounds of disapproval whilst hopping up and down on a branch over hung by his tail. The mink ran in and out of the boulders, through tunnels and under the fallen trunks of trees until, unable to elude his pursuers he slid into the water and swam upstream.

Setra felt the vibrations from the swimming mink which rose to the surface, breathed, paddled on and then dived on top of a small peal which raced across the pool. The mink chased the fish which alarmed others and the salmon waiting to spawn, until the pool milled with frightened fish. The mink caught Setra momentarily in a corner, biting the peal's adipose fin, but the sea trout, heavier by three pounds, thrashed sideways knocking air bubbles from the animal which surfaced, swam to the bank and skulked away to search for mice and voles. The magpie and the jays followed the mink through the wood, their cries growing fainter and then ceasing when he disappeared down a rabbit hole.

Sealass swam between the banks, then settled motionless under the trailing branches of a bush before sidling out to the gravel run-off where she lay on her side thrashing her tail in a foot of water to lift the small stones. She continued at this work, making a shallow redd a hand's width across, the length of her body and with the gravel piled up in a ridge behind. Eggs dribbled from her vent, forced out by the digging effort and the twists and turns made in eluding the mink. The egg sacs inside her body had been ruptured for several days and she now extruded the loose ova in muscular spasms. Setra swung downstream of the hen, nosed forward to lie with her, vibrating his body to release the milt which fertilized the eggs as they sank in the redd. At dusk Sealass covered the ova by flattening the scoop with sweeps of her tail. All night they lay together beneath the overhanging bush whilst a dark trout, a cannibal for many years, nosed for loose eggs. The cannibal was omnivorous: small trout and the fry of salmon were pursued, cornered and taken, newly hatched ducklings, swimming mice and frogs were consumed when seized from below. His body was long, his tail short and tattered in age, and needle teeth lined the edge of the lower jaw. The cannibal took up a waiting position behind Sealass and Setra in the early hours in anticipation of their spawning. Soon after first light Sealass swam to mid-stream and with her dorsal fin cutting through the water surface worked her way along the gulleys to a shallow glide. Setra and the cannibal followed and waited as she made a second redd. As the eggs arrived the cannibal hung behind her tail, pushing and nuzzling with an open mouth to suck in the pink ova—Setra rushed at him open-mouthed, hitting the trout below the belly with his snout, forcing him away before taking up his love lie with his mate. Two more redds she made in completing the life task which left her empty, flaccid and listless. Her body was thin and for three days she remained on the spawning bed waiting for the urge to come to swim down the stream to the main river and from there, helped by the winter rains, regain the sea.

Many dying salmon remained in Gnarled Oak Wood; their bodies drained of energy by the release of eggs and milt were thin, weak and diseased, their skins cracked and leathery, white patches covered their heads. Some lost their grip on life, turned on their flanks and died. Some were pulled from the water by foxes who dragged them away beneath the oak trees to be torn, gulped and chewed. Badgers snuffled them at night and crows and ravens picked the tattered skins by day.

Rain came with a mild west wind in December and Sealass began her return migration to the sea on the rising water. Setra followed, but he was weak, he had not fed for nine months and the rottenness in his jaw was spreading to his body and brain. At times he lost balance, turned on his side, then righted himself to follow Sealass out of Gnarled Oak under the night to the healing sea. The nylon trailed behind him and the mink-bitten adipose fin commenced a slow decay. Sealass passed beneath the netting and barbed wire of a fallen sheep fence which dipped into the water, the barbs festooned with tangled weeds which waved in the current. Setra followed, but the nylon became entangled in the wire and the sea trout's head was jerked back, causing him to flounder below the wire until the nylon became wrapped around his tail. Held tail first to the flow, Setra's gill covers opened and closed weakly, his struggles became spasmodic and he drowned. The hanging body twisted and twirled in the living water, sending up gleams of light from the white belly to startle skimming dippers and catch the eyes of buzzards and ravens as they circled in the sky.

At Christmas I walked to Pengelly's cottage, having it in mind to purchase the property. In his lane I gathered holly with red berries to decorate my house, and on an impulse walked up to Gnarled Oak Wood where he sometimes went to watch the spawning fish. There, attended by a white barn owl which settled to watch from a fence post in the evening light, I remembered our fishing days and idly cast a sprig of holly on the water. The holly drifted away to become entangled in the barbed wire of a straggling sheep fence which crossed the stream and there, below the wire, I saw a great sea trout kelt suspended by the tail.

A white owl still hunts the heathers by Stoney Cross, sea trout fingerlings play in freedom below the sunlit ripples of the water surface mirror, and the river flows unheeding to the sea.

A Salmon on the Worm

H E HAD THE CAN beside him on the ground. In the bottom was a layer of damp moss and onto this he dropped the worms as he dug them out of the heap of well rotted horse manure. Little worms were no use, one needed large ones, preferably those big enough to have flat tails of a pale colour and brownish heads. Such worms were hard to come by, they escaped like lightning or clung to their tunnels only to be pulled clear with patience and by a steady draw. Michael was not happy in his work. He would rather not be seen and dug, so far as was possible, in the shelter of the house away from prying eyes. The trouble was he had been given his orders by his wife, she needed a salmon, there was to be a party and the facts that the river was low and the sun shone interminably out of a clear blue sky would not make the party fail to take place. He could understand her point of view—he was always on a river somewhere or other, wandering about as she put it, but when there was a real need ... Well, as he knew that peace in the house could only be achieved with the help of the humble worm, he continued to dig. All fish like worms; thus he would need a considerable number for the trout would eat most of them, pulling and plucking at his laboriously gained specimens. But he had to admire the size of them from this particular manure heap, some were almost as large as baby grass snakes. He wondered about old Oliver Henley, now with God, fishing companion of Izaak Walton, who wrote in 1653 that Oliver kept his worms in a box in which he anointed them with or drop or two of oil of ivy berries, and this made them 'irresistibly attractive'. The trouble was, Michael didn't think ivy berries were present in July for he knew the woodpigeons ate them in December. No good musing on, he thought, I'd better get it over with, for I know I'll be looking over my shoulder all the time I'm fishing. The rules of the river allowed the use of worms, it was just that he had certain standards of his own and liked to consider himself a fly only man who also did a little spinning in the high waters of the early spring. Worms and prawns, well, one seemed to take unfair advantage of the fish, particularly if you could see the salmon and were able to manoeuvre the worm with the help of a weight so that it waved about in the water current just in front of his nose.

Michael picked up the tin and his rod, slung the salmon net over his shoulder and walked down the hill to the river. He would go to Gilbert's Run, a secluded pool well out of sight of farmers working in the fields and those with nothing else to do but look about the place. He hoped there would be a fish which he could see easily on the bottom, if there were three or four so much the better as he would catch just one, leave the others and this would help to salve his conscience. Peering around the trunk of the ash tree at the head of the pool he looked down into the water. Yes, three fish were there, grey torpedo shapes lying in formation, one in front and two behind on either flank. 'Hm', that's a problem, Michael thought, for the one in front was a grilse of about five pounds and certainly of insufficient bulk to feed the chattering multitudes who would be coming to the party, whilst the two to the rear on either side were sizeable fish. What was worse, the one in front looked hungry and alert, much more so than the larger dormant fellows. The grilse was bound to snatch up the worms before the others stirred from slumber. Still, there was nothing for it, he'd just have to drop the worms in front of them and let the best fish win. Michael knotted on a half ounce weight to the end of his line, then a yard of nylon to which he tied a single hook of generous size. Feeling sorry for the worms he threaded two upon the hook and cast them out. The weight sank quickly to the bottom, the worms waved about downstream in a most enticing manner just in front of the formation of salmon. As predicted the grilse moved forward, opened his mouth, took in the worms and then to his relief, blew them out. The right hand fish, of ample size, moved forward, pushed the grilse to one side and swallowed the bunch of worms. Michael counted five and struck.

The party was a success, it raised the tone for a whole salmon to be upon the table even though, to Michael, its white and baleful eye seemed to look at him in sorrow and contempt, a victim of deceit. He looked up, only to catch the eye of a fishing friend advancing on him across the room. "My word, Mike, bit of luck, that fish in these conditions. Had him at dusk I suppose whilst waiting for the sea trout. What fly?". A fish bone might have stuck in Michael's throat for he turned a salmon pink. "Garden Ranger," he choked, and took a glass of wine.

Giles and the Ancient Dartmoor Trout

THE OLD BROWN TROUT was ugly. His black eel-like body had wasted over many seasons and now terminated in a split and ragged tail. His head had not reduced. The bones of the skull became prominent as the flesh receded, and the hooked undershot jaw was edged with teeth.

He had not always been ugly. At one time, in the distant summers of his youth, his shoulders had been plump and full and red spots had glowed upon his flanks. In the seasons of memory he chased hatching sedge flies as they danced in the sunset, and sucked them down from the rippling surface of the brook.

The waterway meandered off the moor between high banks of black peat. It twisted and twinkled over gravel and, when angry after rain, the water swirled and undercut the banks which collapsed and were swept away. In winter snipe probed the red bogs of the valley and curlew nested there in spring.

Much of the brook was shallow, having been robbed in Drake's day by the Devonport Leat. This stone-lined trench had carried water to fill the casks of the admiral's wooden ships. Thereafter the old trout's ancestors had grown smaller to match the little brook. In one place medieval man had made a granite clapper bridge. Behind the single pier the stream had cut a pot or hole and there the old trout lived. He had chosen well, having the pick of morsels swept by in the channels to either side: dragonfly larvae, a drowned mouse which had fallen off the bank, and careless little trout. Winter is lean on the moor. Insect life is dormant, ravens move to hunt the low-ground farms, and frogs have not yet spawned. Salmon dug redds in the gravel above the bridge to lay their eggs, and the old trout dug up the spawn. When the salmon ova hatched, the alevins emerged to continue the cycle of life, they too kept him alive. But it did not continue so. False moves are sometimes made in the game of life, and as his grandfather said to Giles, who came to stay on Dartmoor with his trout rod in the holidays: "Don't forget, boy, in time they all make a mistake". He made this observation to encourage his grandson who had pitted his wits against the trout in the Easter holidays. The trout had never been deceived and now it was the end of the August holidays and the new school term approached. Giles had often pitched his fly under the bridge where it alighted, light as gossamer, to float beside the old trout's hole. Over the fish would stroll, lock on to it with a suspicious eye, back down beneath the floating morsel, then turn away. Giles had trembled at the thought that his mouth might open—but it never did. Grandpa said in early April "Send him a grannom" and at the May half-term "Try a black long-legged hawthorn fly". The trout rejected them all.

In the yard of Grandpa's farm there existed for many years a cockerel which awoke the boy soon after dawn with loud and penetrating calls. The bird was bristly of neck, long of spur, and though full of fight and courage was lost to a passing fox. Reynard left a trail of feathers on the track to the wood where Giles found the bird's head and neck. He plucked some feathers from the neck to use in the dressing of an artificial sedge. With the hook in the fly vice he wound them on to the shank, adding an inch of tinsel, a twist of red silk and a spot of glue. It was a good fly; a mouthful of substance; an imitation of the great red sedge. Surely the trout had crushed and tasted with appreciation many such plump bodies.

The old trout had basked all day in the warmth of the August sun. His bones had eased and stored the comfort. As the evening light faded he moved out of his hole to take up station below the right hand channel of the bridge. He waited there in the failing light for the great red sedge to hatch. Memories of former summers, when all was warm and sedges fluttered, passed through his dim slow mind, and he remembered how succulent they were to eat. Giles could discern his shadow as he cast his fly up under the bridge. The trout turned himself out to look at it, backed down for an age then, satisfied, opened his mouth and took. As Grandpa said: "Don't forget, boy, in time they all make a mistake".

Catching up with Penrose*

ANYONE WHO HAS FISHED for and caught one or more salmon is an addict who cannot be cured. Even if he fails to catch a fish for many months, or even a year or two years, he will not give up the quest to catch one more. There is no other fish for him which has the same effect. A man may catch many trout and there is then the chance that he will become bored and satiated. The salmon angler always wants one more. He will dream and scheme to satisfy this need, and if he is very old he will say "just one more". But having caught the fish he cannot concede that the final thrill has taken place: he must land another. And so it goes on. And on.

And so it was with Gilbert Penrose, and I am pleased to say still is although he grows more plump and less agile with every final year which passes. He now expends his limited

---

*This is a true account of three salmon caught one morning by the author some years ago on Dartmoor in the days before 'catch and release', and one salmon taken by Penrose whose surname has been changed. Today, conservation is the rule, the first salmon caught must be returned and not more than one or two, at the most, be

64

energy with care, husbanding his strength which is used solely upon the most profitable stretch of the river. Not for him the rocky path or upward hillside climb. And he seems to catch more, for he knows each pot, hole, streamy run and every fishy place. If it wasn't his final year I would become jealous of his success. I ought not to be jealous for he will tell me anything I want to know about the fishing: he will even show me! He is no longer secretive of his methods, but always has one more trick hidden up his sleeve. It is hard to steal a march on him for he doesn't go anywhere other than to this productive stretch of the river, and when he is there he notices everything and catches all the salmon which are willing; one or two which need persuading; some which are difficult or downright unwilling.

Despite his position of superiority we are great friends. There is no reason why he should not be friendly for he is always one, or two, up. The fact that I have good feelings in his direction is due to his corpulence which can, I am sure, harbour no illwill, and to his twinkling humour. He also keeps bees and when I have no salmon, will furnish me with a pot of honey to take home. Even so, in what might be his final year, I felt the need to catch up. Fishing is very competitive and not at all idle as is imagined by those outside the brotherhood.

I therefore awaited my chance which could only come with the arrival of the grilse in July and much rain. If the river ran full and strong at dawn, which would be at five o'clock in the morning, one or two might be caught before he was about. Thus when the rain came and the river rose I was on the bank soon after sunrise tying on a fly in which I have confidence. It is a great fly, this pattern, dressed as a tube with a treble hook in a socket in the tail. Being mostly orange I can see the lure as it is swept across the river. This visibility keeps me full of expectation that a pair of opening jaws will follow and then snap shut and the salmon will be mine. He will only be mine if the strike is delayed. He must be given time to turn down, then I feel for the pull and bang home the hooks by a firm lifting of the rod.

All these things were done correctly when the first salmon rose that early morning. Within seven minutes he was on the bank, a fine cock fish of seven pounds. Tying him nose to tail with a piece of twine I carried him by this handle to the next pool on the productive stretch of water: Penrose piece. The place is not really a pool at all, for in dry weather the depth is only a foot or two, but on that morning with a stain of peat in the river and an extra foot in the level the fish rested there, just for an hour or two on their way up-river.

The second salmon came at six o'clock in a lovely rolling curve full of dash and determination. He would have it and no other fish be allowed to take the fly. I gathered him to me with pleasure and satisfaction. Penrose was being caught up, or so I thought, and if a third could be caught we would be equal for that season—so far as the season had progressed.

A third salmon was hooked and landed, though much against his will for he became very cross with me. He jumped many times, even once on to the far bank from which I was able to pull him back into the river, although with grass upon the leader. He twisted the line around underwater rocks, and as soon as it was freed set off downstream; he wouldn't stop. As I caught up with him in one pool he would dash out of the tail into the next. He didn't exactly wait for me to catch up but he didn't out distance me to the extent that hope would be lost. In the end I slyly manoeuvred myself below him and as he swam downstream to pass me intercepted him with the net and scooped him out. He was a brave fish this salmon which brought me level with Penrose at 10 o'clock in the morning. I sat for a while on the bank to admire the catch and regain my breath. With no need to fish on, I made my way slowly upstream towards my car a mile distant.

When he is fishing Penrose wears a small blue woollen cap, knitted by his wife. It has no brim and it would not be surprising to find that it was his bedcap, and when the time arrives to fish he just rises, pulls on his clothes and makes his way to the river, wearing his bedcap. It doesn't have a tassle with a woolly bobble on the end or one could be certain of the night time use. You do not easily discern him as he fishes down the river, for he looks much like an old round stunted bush, with two branches sticking out as arms. But the blue cap is a giveaway, protruding above the undergrowth. As I made my way up-river there was this cap on top of the Penrose bush. With his rod beside him he was seated on a rock close to the river which still ran at a most inviting height. He motioned me to sit beside him on the rock and there we shared a tin of beer and ate some sandwiches. He was full of good cheer about my salmon for he never begrudges anyone a fish, having caught so many himself.

As we sat he said "There's a salmon below that rock over there. I've risen him". When we had completed our snack he raised himself with rheumaticy care "Must be on my way, there's a beehive I have to move at home, but I'll just take that fellow with me".

The salmon's head came up as the fly swam above the fish in a narrow gap between the rocks—and went down without a take. Twice more Penrose moved the fish with the passing lure. Changing tactics, he left the fly swimming above the salmon's resting place, moving the lure upstream a couple of feet, then letting it drop back the same distance. On the fourth upstream draw the salmon took. "Ah ha" said Penrose, then trotted off downstream to an area of slack water to await the arrival of the salmon. In time the fish followed, persuaded by the current and the steady pull of the rod, and was netted. "If they wished I used to let them go down first," he said, "that was ten years ago when I could skip after them, but I'm not so nimble now, so I take my time and arrive first".

After he left the water ran away, the river fell, the salmon returned to a state of torpor and Penrose remained one up.

Salmon Poachers and Prawns

IT WAS HARD FOR the Justices to be impartial in the matter for two of them fished for salmon and the third, the local vet, felt ill disposed toward any person causing suffering to animal, fish or fowl.

The chairman, Henry Berkeley, cleared his throat and, to the man in the dock, seemed to swell slightly in size, particularly his red-veined face and bulging eyes. The subject of Henry's gaze fixed his attention on the clock at the back of the court whilst waiting for the sentence to be imposed by the beak who reminded him of a well fed frog. The slack skin under Henry's chin swelled as he spoke and the leader of the salmon poaching gang expected a burping, froglike croak to be ejected. Henry was winding himself up, anyone could see that, and 'Creeper' Martin feared the worst. When it came the sentence was not too bad: a £200 fine for himself, £150 each for his two mates, the net and their van forfeit. With 'time to pay' he'd hardly feel the pinch for the three of them took a value of fish from the rivers in a good week which would more than cover the fines; the net was not expensive, and the van had spent the prime of life working for the Post Office.

After the hearing Creeper returned to his village house where he rested for a day or two, purchased another van, a replacement net and took walks along the public footpaths bordering the rivers. Pools were watched for signs of fish, places where a gill net could be stretched across the river memorized, getaway tracks noted and secluded lanes to hide the van were found. He didn't regard his way of life as crooked or a waste of time for he enjoyed the excitement, there was money in the game, and it was a way of evening the odds with those born to a station above his own. The bosses fished by day for salmon which came up from the sea—anybody's fish below the tidal mark. What was the difference in ownership when they arrived in the river? He would take his share and, as there was no other way, help himself at night.

A month after the poaching case Henry Berkeley rested on a deck chair outside the fishing hut at the top end of his water, which was one and a half miles of double bank salmon river. Twenty yards upstream a wooden bridge marked the upper limit of his beat which was in an area of the river on which all the owners of fisheries had agreed a 'fly only' rule. Henry's fly rod was propped prominently against the wall of the hut where it would be clearly visible to anyone passing along the public right of way along the other bank. The rod was a highly varnished split cane, and the fly (which had not seen the inside of a salmon's mouth) a florid example of the dresser's art.

Henry basked in the sun, raising himself from time to time to trundle to the river from which he withdrew a bottle of tonic water to dilute, slightly, the gin which flowed from his flask into a silver cup. He sighed with satisfaction whilst squeezing drops of lemon juice onto the slices of purchased smoked salmon which he had brought to the river. Life was good, for even though the sun shone down, making fishing an unrewarding toil, a man could eat, drink and sleep.

Henry shelled another prawn, a dish of which accompanied him on his fishing days together with brown bread and butter. He ate with appreciation, then wiped his fingers on a white cloth in which his food had been wrapped. He settled himself more comfortably in the chair, placed a cushion behind his lead and with his cap pulled over his eyes drifted off to sleep.

The peace of this idyllic scene was shattered by a splosh which caused Henry to raise his bulging rheumy eyes to the river and there, above the bridge, a ring of widening waves marked the place where a salmon had jumped clear to bash down upon the placid surface of the smoothly flowing river. Henry, who was not given to urgent decisions, considered the position. The fish was in the water of Major Overstone who was on holiday in Iceland. Overstone, being very much a fly only man, went there annually in July to exercise his skill. The salmon would be two dozen yards above the bridge beneath which was a sandy patch on which the Major sometimes beached a fish, having brought it down from the lie above. Henry mulled over the pros and cons. The fly would be no good at lunch time on so bright a day, but why had God invented prawns and placed them close to hand? Henry succumbed.

It was the work of minutes to unwind the dressing of the salmon fly, discard the gaudy feathers but retain the silk which held the fly together. With this he bound a plump and glistening prawn to the hook, concealing the shank between the legs and tucking the eye of the hook under the prawn's tail from which the nylon now emerged. He cut a sliver of lead from the sheeting on the roof of the hut, nipped the weight onto the cast a yard above the prawn, then ambled up the river. As he came level with, then passed the

bridge, he looked about with apprehension and a weight of guilt descended on his shoulders. He wished he hadn't made a start but he seemed to have no control over his legs which forced him on.

The salmon was obliging, taking the prawn on his second cast and Henry was able to work him down to the sandy patch under the arches of the bridge, beach him and knock the fish upon the head. Thank goodness that was over. He straightened his back to see with horror a head peering at him over the wooden edge of the arch above the sandy place. The owner of the head had clearly arrived there by walking down the public footpath along the other bank. "'Allo guvnor. Wot's yer game? Tut tut, a lil poaching' eh an' wat's this 'ere—a prawn? Dear me, not at all the thing, we 'ave come unstuck 'aven't we. An' wot'll the Major say?" Henry paled, then blustered "Now see here, be off with you. It's none of your business and in any case I have the Major's permission. I know you, you're the poacher—what's your name?" "Creeper, guvnor. That's who I am, Creeper. An' that's 'ow I caught yer at yer lil game. Permission you may 'ave to fish but permission you 'ave not got fer that there lil red prawn. In't ee luvly, all red an' plump an' juicy. I can see you be a real judge o' prawns". Henry groaned. "Don't take on so my deah chap," said Creeper in a comforting tone. "The Major now, ee can't do nufink 'cos ee aint 'ere. That is ee can't do nufink unless I tells 'im, an' why should I do that? I looks to the future Guv—sort of like an insurance it is to 'ave a friend upon the bench. One good turn deserves another I says—an' doubtless you agrees". The abyss in front of Henry opened wider and deepened. It was blackmail. Agree, or he would be ruined. It would never come to court of course. The most that would actually happen would be an embarrassing wigging over the telephone from Overstone—but the prawn was in another category entirely. His integrity would be lost and he would have to retire from the riparian owners association. His word as a gentleman would no longer be accepted. It would be horrible. He couldn't think why he had been tempted. He perspired, his shoulders crumpled and shook as deep sobs came from his chest. He felt a heavy pain behind his ribs and then a crack on the head as he stumbled and fell against a bridge support. What was happening? Somebody was shaking him. He found himself lying on the ground beside his chair. "You alright Guv?" asked a voice. "I was watchin' yer orf th' bridge an' you was thrashing' about an' moanin' somethink terrible. Spot of indigestion I reckons". Henry looked up at the man—it was that poaching chap Creeper. He looked beyond him to the rod where he was relieved to see the fly stuck in the cork of the butt. There was no sign of a prawn; he must have been scheming up the plan as he dozed; he had often thought of slipping on a prawn if no one was about.

Creeper looked at him and winked. "There's a fish just jumped above the bridge in the Major's water. Why not 'ave a go fer 'im Guvnor?". The man glanced at the dish. "You got zum nice lil prawns 'ere, now why don't you trot one past 'im, ee mid catch 'old m'dear".

The Adventures of a
Sea Trout

THE WILL TO LIVE now left her, the driving urge slowed as she extruded the final pearly eggs into the gravel bed of her spawning redd. With the last of them gone, fertilised by the shed milt of a small cock sea trout, she turned her empty, flaccid body to swim down river to the sea.

White fungus covered her head which was too large for the thin, wasted body with split and ragged tail. For a while she maintained direction downstream, moving a little faster than the current, but soon the water overtook her, rolled over the feebly swimming body and washed her down towards the sea.

A badger which found the stranded fish ate the pale and tasteless flesh in the night and the head he left was picked clean the next morning by crows and magpies. A raven watched the feast from high in the cold December sky but he did not descend, because men were active close by fixing a metal plate to a block of granite.

The bronze plaque recorded the names of those responsible for the completion of the dam which would store the rains of winter and flood the valley in which the sea trout spawned. The impounded waters would meet the requirements of the citizens of south Devon towns during the dry weeks and months of summer.

The dam was closed; the waters rose, covering a farm road and a bridge which crossed the sea trout stream. A place of beauty was recreated less beautiful than before. The river below the dam became a trickle of compensation water, the bed silted, bushes and weeds grew down the banks to choke the living soul of the stream whose termination after thousands of years was recorded on the metal plate.

Above the level of the enclosed water the stream lived on. The sea trout eggs hatched in spring into tiny alevins complete with a sustaining yolk sac from whose nourishment the fishes grew slowly to fingerling size, henceforth to be fed meagrely by the pure waters of Dartmoor. These waters tumbled freely down, to be impounded by the reservoir and the water pipes of the far-off town.

The bright sea trout fingerlings moved down the stream into the still waters above the dam where the newly flooded ground provided rich feeding. Unaware of the life sentence imposed upon them in the reservoir by the mayor and corporation of the town, the fingerlings played freely in the morning sun which lit the moving mirror of the surface waves above their heads.

They chased each other in and out of the submerged granite walls of the now abandoned farm and the hut circles of earlier Bronze Age men. Their birthright now taken from them, was to go down river to the sea, to feed and grow strong and then return in muscular maturity to the river of their birth to spawn.

Months passed and their numbers declined—the heron took his toll along the water's edge in the early dawn, and others were sucked to a black, lightless death in the contraptions of the dam installed by the minions of the mayor.

Some of the peal fingerlings (for that is the name of a Devon sea trout) continued to grow in silver streamlined beauty, reaching sizes of 12 to 14 inches, to be caught on flies at the water's edge by startled brown trout fishermen.

In winter the constant rains raised the level of the water and dark waves overflowed the dam to be transformed into white and silver pearls of spraying beauty falling 50 feet to the dam pool below. With these pearls went a solitary ten-inch peal, sole survivor of the darting shoal of fish.

Bruised and gasping he lay quietly on the bottom of the pool below the waterfall. His gills and mouth opened and closed slowly, absorbing the life-giving oxygen of the now well-aerated waters. Slowly, the peal's strength returned and the magnet of the ocean reached him from the far-off sea.

Slipping out of the pool, the survivor made his way down the trickling remnant of the ancestral river trail. Farther down the valley other streams joined the waterway which grew in size and slowed somewhat in speed. Wild March daffodils lined the meadowy banks, dippers bobbed white waistcoats on the river rocks and woodpeckers flew in looping flight. The sea trout followed the gentler watercourse until his body was welcomed by the healing salt waters of the sea.

For three years the peal followed the ocean currents of the North Atlantic. He grew strong. His tail changed from forked to square, his shoulders thickened and fat lodged between the pink flakes of his muscles. In June his milt sacs, now filled with sperm, itched within his belly and he drove his six-pound body irritably through the seas until the moment when a water molecule fresh with the aroma of the Devon stream entered his mouth and the magnet pulled, this time for home as he entered the river through the estuary.

Eight miles up the river valley from the sand bars at its mouth, or seven as the cormorant flies, in the slumbering village of Buckland Magna stood Buckland House, a Georgian home of unpretentious size with whitewashed walls, slate roof and stables rotting in disuse. The lawn of this house sloped down to Monk's Pool on the river. The owner was a widower, 80 years old and stooped and slow. Arthritis knobbled his fingers and he found it difficult to tie on his salmon and sea trout flies.

The old man's pleasures were limited to his study which looked over the lawn to the river, the company of his black Labrador, Snuff and, on his better days, to fishing for sea trout after dusk for an hour or two. Sometimes he just sat and recalled and waited in the warm comfort of June evenings. The dog followed the example of his master whom he guarded with watchful eyes.

On a pine table in his study were a fly-tying vice, scissors, feathers, fur, silks and varnishes. This outfit had been given to him at Christmas, but he was reluctant to make a start by following the instructions in the little book in case he found his fingers too infirm, or eyesight more dimmed by age than he would care to admit to himself. But the plunge had to be taken, so he sat on the stool, turned on the Anglepoise lamp and fixed a Number Eight hook in the vice.

A simple fly was the answer—just a silver body and a black wing, then he would have made a start and other flies would follow. It proved to be easier than he had thought possible—the fly seemed just the right weight and size. Yes, there was no doubt it would be accepted by the peal—a good and simple fly. There was really no difficulty. He would make another for his grandson who sometimes came to stay with him.

It seemed that it would never grow dark that evening as the old man sat on his bench beside Monk's Pool. His rod was set up, with the fly and nylon of his cast soaking in a little pool at the river's edge. He had seen three bats flit by—for as long as he could remember he had always waited to see three before judging it dark enough to start. He must remember to tell his grandson about the bats. A fine boy, his grandson, who fished for trout in the moorland burns and ate them for his breakfast.

By Jove, that was a big peal. The old man heard a heavy splash and saw the waves where a sea trout had jumped clear of the water and bashed down again. He slipped softly into the water and felt his way along the bottom in his waders. He made three short casts, laying the line gently on the water.

No splash, no noise, and then a quiet and steady pull as the survivor took his fly. The old man raised his rod and slipped. They found him next morning, face down in the water, waders full, the rod clutched in stiffened fingers. There was no fly.

That evening Snuff sat alone beside the water and whined from time to time. The old man's daughter saw a great sea trout jump several times as she came to fetch the dog to the house. Perhaps there was something wrong with the fish, it did seem to have something black in its mouth, but there were already bats about and you could not see clearly.

The Chalkstream Pike

THE MALLARD DUCK had placed her nest in an indentation in the top of a pollarded willow tree which grew on the river bank. She had flown many times into the flattened crown taking with her beakfuls of dried grass and leaves which she worked into a bowl, the inside being lined with her own down. For four weeks she incubated the nine buff-coloured eggs during which period the slender shoots growing from the crown of tree sprouted pale green leaves. By the end of the incubation the screen around her gave privacy to the hatching ducklings and, with the exception of a single addled egg, the shell splitting was complete and all the ducklings dry to leave the nest within two days. The mother then dropped down onto the gently flowing water below and, encouraged by maternal quacks, the little ones plunged too to bounce like corks upon the surface of the trout waters of The Chalkley Piscatorial Society. The duck led her brood upstream close to the cover of rushes growing at the edge of the muddy bank where she dibbled for food at the stems of water plants, encouraging the tiny balls of fluff to follow her example.

Close by the duck nest tree and adjacent to the river a wooden black- tarred hut gave shelter to trout fishermen. Each day two or three placed their lunch bags on the central wooden table and ate on benches set against the walls. The front of the shelter had no door at the entrance, on either side of which were glassless windows where old men could sit to watch for rising trout.

The senior members of the Society took up lunchtime station in the hut at places on the bench which they claimed by right of long usage, convenience to the table being important and from where, without craning the neck, a good view might be had of the river. Discussion of the morning activity took place, catches were admired and prospects considered for the evening.

In the corner of the hut closest to the river sat 'Heron' Blakey, a thin tall elder of the Society whose habit was to stand quite still beside the river observing the rising trout and then, after half-an-hour when a suitable victim had been discerned, Heron would deceive the trout with a well placed and chosen fly. Even in the hut the Heron's head poked above the window sill and today his prominent Adam's Apple bobbed with agitation for in midstream he saw a fish rise to a mayfly. Every five or six minutes thereafter the nose broke the surface to engulf a fly, a broad back slid through the surface in an oily fashion and the disappearing tail waved momentarily before sinking from view—and what a tail! The Heron blinked and discreetly turned aside for there must be no competitors in the catching of this fish. The other members talked and ate—they had not seen the trout. The Heron nonchalantly chewed a final biscuit with a lump of cheese, drank a cup of coffee without apparent haste and went outside, picking up his rod from the rack where it rested against the wall of the

hut. The yellow mayfly tied to the end of the leader was to his satisfaction.

He had been much troubled in the morning by the duck which followed him and whose brood of ducklings ate the mayflies as they hatched, scuttled across the surface to grab the drifting insects. Several times the Heron had pulled his imitation away in time to save a deceived duckling from the hook. The trout rose again, the Heron cast his fly and as a duckling scuttling over the surface to take his offering there was a monstrous swirl beyond the trout, a pair of jaws emerged and smacked shut upon the duckling. The trout, taking fright, shot off upstream, the water calmed, and all that remained was a curled yellow feather which drifted away on the current. The Heron was outraged, a pike, and what a pike, in the gentle waters of the Society! He could imagine it hiding in the weeds with long flat shovelled jaws, cold up-turned eyes and yellow greenish flanks. So persistent an eater of trout must be caught at once by any means available. He even felt sorry for the duck whose brood was

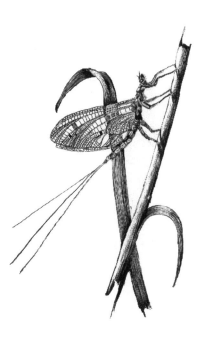

being depleted by the monster. Consternation shook the resting members in the hut—this fish must be at least 10 lb, the Heron said. There hadn't been so large a pike in the water since the '30s when 'Sneaker' Clifford had caught one on a large salmon fly which he had been using to tempt the fattest trout of the mill pool. The matter was not mentioned in front of non-members for only small imitative dry flies were allowed upon the Chalkley waters. Sneaker had failed to be re-elected to the Committee and shortly afterwards resigned.

The Society purchased two pike traps, wire cages into which a pike might swim when travelling up the channels between the beds of weed. Nothing was caught other than a dabchick which swam into the cage and drowned. May and June passed without a sighting but trout seemed scarce.

Some grumbled, saying things were not as they used to be, and attributing the scarcity to poor stocking by the Committee. Some doubted the Heron's tale. The Heron himself grew thinner with worry, spending long hours peering at the water, only his head protruding above the rushes. The matter was revived dramatically when a guest, playing a trout in the mill pool, had the fish snatched from him at the net. The trout was flashing about just below the surface when the pike surged by, taking the trout with him. The guest had played the captor for a while but the leader broke and the pool settled again to tranquillity. The miller's boys no longer bathed in the swirling waters, fearful of the murky depths and the chance of bitten toes and fingers.

The pike was unaware of the members' vengeful thoughts. Nothing had changed his life which had been spent almost entirely in the mill pool. He had commenced his growth in the shallows of a nearby lake where he had been trapped and placed in a jam jar by Thumper Herbert, the bully of the village boys. On his way home carrying the jam jar and a bowl of frog spawn Thumper had come across a smaller boy innocently fishing with a worm in the mill pool. Thumper, who regarded the area as his own preserve when fishermen were not about, caught the poacher, tucked his head under his left arm and punched his nose. As the boy still howled defiance his face was thrust into the water several times whilst the frog spawn and the pickerel were emptied over him. Satisfied with the abject state of the victim Thumper continued home, whilst the pickerel took up a wary, protected position beneath a lily in the shallows.

The first victims of the pike were minnows, the nymphs of insects and other small and creeping things. As his size increased he turned to frogs, trout, crayfish and the young of ducks and moorhens. In maturity a trout of a pound or two was taken once or twice a week, and in between meals he rested in the channels of the weeds at the edges of the pool.

The Heron sought the advice of the tackle dealer in the town. "Spin for him" he was told, "no pike can resist a wobbling plug dragged across the entrance to his lair". The Heron tried, but apart from hooking a good-sized trout he had no success. The pike displayed no desire to chase the plug across the pool when all it had to do was take a gently cruising trout or slow succulent frog. The Heron returned to the tackle dealer who sold him a large single hook and sent him to the fishmonger, a pike fishing friend of his. The fishmonger had no scruples as to method. His instructions were clear. "Pass the 'ook through the lips of a 'erring, cast it out and leave it on the bottom of the pool. When you feel the blighter take it let 'im get it in 'is guts—then strike 'ard". The Heron cast out as he was told and waited on the bank. The pike smelt the herring as the oily aroma curled around the pool on the circulating currents. He left his hole to eye the dead fish resting on the mud, his fins moved him slowly forward until, opening his mouth, he took the herring across his jaws. The Heron waited, his head above the reeds. The pike turned slowly, crossed the pool, and reversing into his hole, opened his jaws to turn the herring's head towards his stomach as the Heron struck—too soon. The bait was plucked out of the bony jaws and flying through the air landed in the branches of an overhanging tree where it dangled, swaying in the breeze for all to see as evidence of failure.

The solution came to the Heron one afternoon in August whilst driving through the village. He saw brass rabbit wires suspended on a nail driven into the wall outside the fishing tackle and gun shop. Why hadn't he thought of it before? He

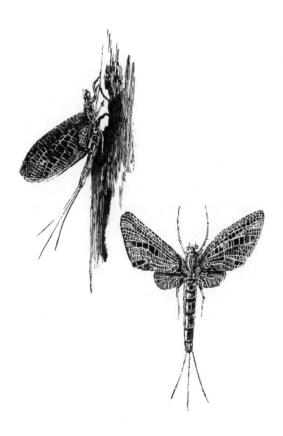

would snare the pike whilst the fish basked near the surface in the summer sun. The Heron purchased a snare which he attached to a stiff piece of wire three feet in length, and this he wrapped around the end of the pole with which his wife propped up the clothes line in the garden.

Taking his outfit to the river he peered through the rushes and there, sunning himself a foot below the surface was the pike. The fish was very large and it seemed to the Heron that all his fins were at the tail end—just as though his pants had slipped. Pushing the pole slowly through the rushes he sank the noose into the water upstream of the fish and then moved it carefully over his snout, passed his eyes and gills then, when half way down his length the Heron heaved. The wire tightened around the belly of the fish which flew through the air to land, snapping his jaws upon the bank. The Heron fell heavily upon his enemy, beating the bony skull with a priest. Breathing fast he stood back in triumph and was joined by the miller's sons who stood around in awe. The youngest, a pale child of seven or eight years, removed his thumb from his mouth to look upwards at the Heron. "Hey mister," he piped, "that's a good un i'n't it. Thumpers 'elpin ee ain ee. I zeed 'im, yesterday I zeed 'im, 'ee put in zum more pikes for ee".

The Chub Fly and the
Salmon: A Salmon Story

THE GREY AND PORTLY CHUB knew by now almost all those things which were important for his survival in a deep, slow-running stream. He knew the best spot to be by the water entrance to his pool through which food morsels came to sustain his aldermanic three-pound bulk, and he occupied that place. He knew the safest hole in the pool and went there rather ponderously when danger threatened, gently displacing by his bulk any small chub in residence. He made no mistakes, took no risks, tolerated no usurpers and in a contented restful sort of way just grew steadily larger.

A pollarded willow tree grew on the bank of the pool. It was an old tree whose roots on one side were washed by the stream which undercut the bank, and in these roots the fishes of the stream took refuge in times of danger. A boy of 12 or 13 years sat hidden in the knobbly crown of the tree one day in June. Well-shielded by the leaves he made his preparations. From his pocket he took a tin on which he had written 'chub flies'—he knew they were chub flies as the packet he had purchased in the shop said so. The flies were black and rather too bushy and were the only flies he possessed. In fact they were the only thing he had at the moment to fish with, having left school in a hurry for the river. The boy would have preferred a bumble bee or grasshopper impaled upon a hook but had not had time to catch one after his lessons. He tied the fly to the leader on his rod which was camouflaged by the branches. Peering down into the pool he watched in fascination as the alderman engulfed a green and squirming caterpillar which had slowly descended onto the water at the end of a silken thread. 'Crikey, if only I could get him. Good job I've got my best leader on the rod', he thought as he gently pushed the tip out through the leaves.

The alderman had enjoyed the caterpillar. The skin enclosed more meat and juice than spindly flies, which he found unsatisfactory, being mostly wings and legs. Give him a plump worm or caterpillar any day. He looked up hopefully, cocked his head a little to one side, and was surprised to see a further meal descending on another silken thread. The meal looked like a fat black spider and the chub watched it greedily but without much hope; spiders could go up as well as down, he knew, but he moved a little closer—just in case. The boy's heart thundered as the fish lifted in the water and he dropped the fly with a plop on the placid surface of the stream. There was a bulging swirl, thick white lips engulfed the fly, the line tore off the reel as the alderman realised his mistake and made for the safe place.

The boy slid down the tree, barking knees and forearms, and rushing into the tail of the pool, drew the chub away from the refuge. The battle was short, sharp and final.

'Crumbs', thought the boy, who was going to Scotland in the holidays, 'if they work on chub, what about salmon?' The enormity and ambition of this thought stunned him. For a moment he became still in reverie. A picture then floated into his mind of a triumphal return to the grown-ups at the shooting lodge with the 'King of Fish' in his arms. It was all quite clear and obvious—he knew it could be done.

In Scotland, at the mouth of the Sula river, a seal's head rose above the surface of the salt waters of the sea. The seal blew and sighed after his dive and looked about with large and filmy eyes. His whiskers dripped and steamed with the warmth of his breath on the cold dawn air. It was the middle of July on the West coast, the run of small one sea-winter salmon, were entering the river on the flood tide. The seal had killed two, taking a bite from the swimming fish which then wobbled on erratically to fall away, sink and die, to the delight of crabs and lobster which feasted on the rich pink flesh. Other salmon, alarmed by the thudding shocks of the chase, shot forward in powerful upriver flight into the Sea Pool. The seal would not follow into the fresh peaty water and turned away to swim to Seal Island in the Sound. He hauled himself out onto the rocks to sleep and bask in the rising sun.

Old Donald saw a silver grilse leap in Sea Pool as he pushed his bicycle along the path beside the river and then a second fish of about 10 lb showed at the neck of the pool as it searched the way upstream. The old man nodded to himself with approval; it had always been so, spring tides on the flood brought in the fish, and if there was a spate as well, so much the better, for there would be no holding them for four or five miles in one go. Donald hitched the mail bag higher on his shoulder and continued up the valley to Shiel Lodge. He always walked up the valley to see the deer, a grouse or two and sometimes a blackcock in the field by the silver birches. He never saw much if he rode up the valley to deliver the letters, for his bicycle squeaked and grated, he had his head down, and, anyway, it was too much of a pull. Perhaps this afternoon he would have an hour or two on the river himself at Shiel Lodge if the tenants didn't mind.

For the boy the first day of the Scottish holiday had passed in a rush of activities. He had seen a deer before breakfast and a red squirrel had been chased up a tree by a dog. He went to the moor with the guns, but rain stopped the shoot at lunch time when the party returned to the house. The rain continued and the river rose in the late afternoon. Brown trout tucked themselves under the banks to escape the pressure of the peaty water and were passed by salmon and sea trout on their way upstream. Some travelling fish leaped with joy as each new pool was entered on their spawning run, others jumped to knock off the sea lice clinging with tiny suckers to their flanks.

Later the rain ceased, and, having escaped from the house, the boy sat on a stump beside the river and watched the surface of the waters, his chin cupped in his hand. All the fish he saw seemed large to him, even the smaller sea trout which were called finnock in that part. There was too much water now, he was sure of that. Grandpa always said you had to wait for a spate to drop a bit. Perhaps it would be all right in the morning. Pity Grandpa wasn't here; he would know what to do to catch a salmon. Still, he had the chub fly.

The thought of the fly sent him scurrying home to prepare for fishing in the morning. He would have a go with the fly, give it a swim, as he had heard a keeper say. His rod really did not look strong enough and even his best leader hardly seemed up to the envisaged task, and as for the reel, it only had twenty-five yards of line upon it. He pulled off all the line and stretched it out behind the house; it really wasn't enough. He was certain salmon fishers had more line upon their reels, eighty or ninety yards he had heard some say. What about joining on the mackerel spinning line? Thirty pounds breaking strain was sure to be enough. He added twenty yards of this, joining the two sections with a bulky blood knot. All was ready for the morning and if he caught a fish he would land it somehow, by beaching, or grab it around the knuckle of the tail, or with his fingers in the gills. It could be done. The boy's breath came a little faster at the thought. He didn't eat much supper nor sleep too well that night.

The black fly swung on the current across the pool to hang below the rock on which the boy was crouched. It would not sink properly being too bushy. Fish were there without doubt; he had seen two salmon leap below the rock to crash down with such a splash that he felt even more doubtful of his tackle, and he was having difficulty in casting 'down and across' against the upstream wind which pushed at the downstream water flow and made great waves. He tried again during a lull. Out went the cast across the river and, as he raised his rod a little to retrieve, a gust of wind caught the line, whisking it upstream, causing the fly to scuttle over the surface of the rough, black water. A humping, sweeping, shining back-curve of salmon intercepted the skidding fly and took it down. The boy let out a shout, the short, sharp sound ejected from him without thought. The rod bent, the reel screeched, the line accelerated fast, and then he jumped—all the silver length and beauty of him. There was a chance, he knew there was a chance; the pool was not large, perhaps with twenty-five yards of line ...

But what about the knot to the mackerel backing? He mustn't let it go that far. The salmon came back below the boy, who held the rod with trembling arms, all of him shook and his legs were weak. He shifted to ease his knees indented by the rock and in moving pulled the salmon off balance in the water current. The fish shot off downstream, out of the pool and down through the rapids. The boy followed as best he could, stumbling over rocks. The fly line was out, the knot, thank goodness, passed through the rings without jamming and the mackerel line now took the strain. The boy came level with the fish again and reeled in as far as the mackerel knot 'The Knot! The bloody Knot!' the boy called out in sobbing despair, the knot would not come back through the top ring and the salmon was coming close to him.

'Eh, laddie, ye're in a terrible finckle', said the slow and kindly voice of Donald of the Mail, 'but he's almost done, slack off a wee bitty.' The old man had heard the crying shout as he pushed his bicycle along the nearby road and now, beside the boy, gently took the sagging line between his rough and calloused fingers. The salmon was done. Donald drew on the line, beached the fish and pushed it firmly up the shelving sandy bank. 'Dap him on the haed', he told the boy, 'never let a fush be sufferin, yer granfer would'na like ut'.

The postman removed the fly from the salmon's mouth and turned it over in his thick strong fingers. 'A mite fuzzy maybe, but ye never noo wi' saumon.'

The Coming of the Otters

THE TERRITORY OF AQUATA the bitch otter centred on a
derelict marshy length of the river valley. On one side of
the marsh the river ran swiftly, with many twists and turns
which altered from time to time as the water undercut the
banks which collapsed onto the slate bed of the watercourse.
The small river was not deep; it ran fast over the stones due
to a steep fall in the descent from the moor above, and a
lack of weeds and water plants which would have slowed
the flow. There was little mud in which water vegetation
might root, few insects, shrimps or caddis larvae and in
consequence the trout were small and always hungry. In
contrast to the bareness of the watercourse the edges of
the river were lined by blackberry bushes, nettles, brambles
and trees. The roots of this growth held together the stones
and sandy earth of the steep banks, extended out below
the grass of the fields, and where the water had washed
at the bases of the trees and roots trailed in the water.
Aquata searched the roots for trout which hid between the
blackened underwater fingers. In summer leaves formed a
canopy over the bed of the watercourse, cutting out the sun,
and this further discouraged weed growth in the river.

Along the watercourse, separated by shallow stickles, were pools in which Aquata hunted. In places winter storms had caused trees to fall across the stream, forming bridges from bank to bank. The tangled trunks and branches kept out wandering cattle and fishermen, whilst providing secluded refuges for the otter.

In Victorian times, when works were done by men and horses, a ditch had been dug across the marsh to drain the sodden land. Round clay pipes one foot across were laid to the river to discharge the waters of the marsh. The system worked well for many years but after two generations some pipes collapsed blocking the tunnel, and a tree fell sideways on the water's edge breaking the final pipe which became hidden below the fallen trunk. In April Aquata investigated this slender, dark protected hole; crept up the pipe for twenty feet, came to a collapsed section and dug upwards to emerge after a night's work under a bramble patch. She poked her whiskered muzzle above the ground, scrambled out and found herself in a small dry cavity which had been used in the winter by a buck rabbit. The patch had several entrances protected by bramble creepers and stinging nettles. Two nights after the digging she returned to the holt to enlarge the central room under the canopy of thorns. She carried in the dried grasses and reeds of the march to line the floor of the nursery, for here she planned to have the cubs which squirmed within her belly.

She had mated in December in the cold waters of a disused quarry after a courtship of several days with a dog otter several pounds heavier than herself. This dog, Greywhisker, patrolled the river from the source in a Dartmoor mire to the junction with the Lewstone Brook. Aquata was the only bitch within his territory—there had been another older bitch but she had died mysteriously of a sickness. This poisoning came from the Dieldrin sheep dips once used by the farmers of the moor and present in the bodies of trout. Small rodents also accumulated the poison from seed corn dressings and the remnants of these chemicals, although no longer used, had gathered in the liver of the bitch otter which had fed upon the fish and rodents. Greywhisker had mated with her twice but no litter had resulted in her infertile state and she had died of cold.

The dog otter found Aquata's spraint beneath the single arch of a stone bridge two miles above the junction of the Lewstone Brook with his own river. The scent she left excited him to swim upstream to the gravel on a sharp bend where she had marked again upon a boulder. He squeaked twice in excitement, the sound carrying upstream to the bitch who was eating a sea trout kelt. This kelt had come up from the sea the previous July, and having spawned in the gravel headwaters of the river had been caught by the otter in the shallows of the river, the level being low after several days of frost. She continued to feed, chewing lumps of fish as he came out of the water, then paused between bites to chitter at him as he approached. Greywhisker sheered off, climbed the bank and rolled under an alder, then returned to the fish which the bitch had left—and ate whilst she drank with her nose below the surface of the pool, washed, groomed then rolled upon the bank where Greywhisker had flattened the frosty grass. Aquata galloped upstream on the stones and gravel of the waterside, then played with the shiny metal top of a milk bottle washed downstream from the bridge over which villagers tipped buckets of rubbish. Greywhisker courted her for several nights in the river and the water-filled disused quarry; he chased her in and out of the woods and water, and now she was heavy with the litter and warned him off, wishing to be alone.

On a cold night under the stars of The Plough she dropped two cubs in the holt beneath the brambles. She licked the grey fur of the blind bodies of the little ones who sought her teats with tiny heavy heads and small pink pads. She fed them, whereupon the babies fell asleep and she left the holt by a rabbit tunnel leading onto the marsh. She caught two frogs beside a stagnant pool turgid with frogspawn and ate the first ravenously. She played with the second before chewing up the meat and bones, then returned to the cubs, curling her body around them in the dark. After a month the cubs' eyes opened and at two months they greeted their mother just outside the bramble patch when she returned to them with an eel—their first solid food. The young otters tasted the strange thing then returned inside the holt where their mother suckled them. At three months, in July, their coats coarsened and they ventured down the pipe to paddle in the shallows where Aquata released a maimed frog into the pool below the pipe and the heaviest cub, a dog, rushed into the water after the creature which swam slowly in a circle. He chewed the frog whilst growling at his sister who later shared the kill. Greywhisker passed the holt at intervals but did not take part in the family life. His time was much taken in keeping a young otter from his territory. The interloper had been born three years earlier two miles downstream of the junction of his river with the Lewstone Brook and had reached an age when he sought an area of his own. Greywhisker marked the limits of his territory regularly,

travelling three or four miles a night, stopping to leave his spraint in prominent places at the river's edge and under road and foot bridges. Being frustrated in his invasion attempt the interloper passed upstream to spend the summer on the trout streams and marshes of the moor.

Aquata and her mate lived on the river for a year before attracting the attention of a man who fished for the little trout. This man occupied with his wife and children a house with walls of slate built long ago in the days of cobs and carts and riding horses. As the children grew he instilled in them an interest in the birds of the valley, the deer, the badgers and the fish. They gathered primroses and wild anemones in the spring along the river banks; raised tadpoles in a pool of water in a ditch behind the house, bird-nested, fished, swam in the river and learned the ways and sounds of the creatures of the valley. The man showed them the grey badger hairs where their noctural paths passed beneath a fence whose barbs scraped their rough and hairy backs, the slots of deer, and bark stripped by them from the trees; the tiny footmarks of the mink and then one day the footprint of an otter. He knew at once the maker of the prints upon the sand and gravel banks, no other creature would leave a pad mark of such a size in such a place. At first he thought it was a solitary travelling otter, but over the weeks as he looked with greater care and frequency he seldom failed to find the tracks. Encouraged, he searched closely, wading down the river on the shifting stones with a staff held in his hand. The scrutiny revealed many details of river life: the rounded dipper's nest of moss with an entrance at the side; a kingfisher flew to her home in a hole bored in the earth under the uprooted bole of a tree. The man looked for the otters' holt but for some days he had to be satisfied with finding droppings on boulders and in the tunnels under the bank above water level. He persisted until one evening, whilst wading thigh deep, a double scat caught his eye. Behind the scats was a hole, the floor of which was smoothed by treading feet. He took one of the scats home to examine it at leisure under a magnifying glass. The teeth and vertebrae of mice, small bones and the shape and size of the scat left no doubt in his mind—an otter visited the hole. A mile further down the river he found a second hole under a jumble of tree stumps pushed there by the farmer's tractor when clearing a field. He found more scats, larger than those by the other holt. Excitement grew—could this be from a dog otter and the smaller ones from a bitch? His youngest child, a slim fair girl of twelve years, found the otters' nursery. She had been attracted by the smoothness of an earthen track close to the fallen tree. She peered under the trunk into the gloom of the broken pipe and drew a damp and heavy smell into her pale nostrils. She called her father who examined the area, noting the underwater direction of the old drain, the bramble patch and the inward leading tunnels.

They saw the otters once. Sitting many yards downwind behind a bush they waited as night fell in September. A dark shadow left a bramble tunnel to move off up the depression of the old drain in the direction of the marsh, and two small bodies emerged briefly to roll upon the grass. With that one sight they had to be content for the grain harvest of the farm was over and the following week a tractor passed that way to obliterate with a whirling machine the hedge tops and the bramble patch. Aquata and the cubs crouched in the pipe unseen and unsuspected as their roof fell in at the tunnel's landward entrance. When night came Aquata led the cubs to the holt of the old tree stumps.

In October rain raised the waters of the stream which subsided after two days leaving the sandbanks smooth and clear. The otters left their footprints, or seal as they are called, on these places and again the fisherman found their holt and was glad. His happiness was replaced by anger as the clearness of the stream became polluted by opaque foul smelling waters. A pig farmer up the valley, short of land on which to spread his sow and fatteners wastes, had led the washings of the buildings to the river which became an evil smelling drain. Other farmers downstream suffered in silence, for one does not betray the misdeeds of another. Who knows—one day a sudden storm might wash the seepage from their silage pits into the stream.

But Aquata left. The cubs went as well to the clearer waters of the Lewstone Brook which ran from wilder lands. The pig farmer mended his ways, but the otters did not return. In time the little trout came back and so did the frogs and dippers, but the kingfisher followed the otters to a cleaner place. The man fished alone, depressed that the otters which had come had now departed. The sandbanks stayed naked of their prints and a mink made foul with his smell the pipe which drained the waters of the marsh.

The Cowman and the Eel

FREDDIE'S UNCLE OWNED a lake stocked with rainbow trout on his dairy farm. The grown-ups fished there with artificial flies in the evenings and had the trout cooked for breakfast the next morning. Sometimes they did not catch anything and then Freddie was asked to do his best to provide the missing breakfasts.

He was staying on the farm for a fortnight of his summer holidays and had set up a tent beside the water to hold his rod, reel and line, hooks and net. Not for him artificial flies, give him a wriggling worm on a hook any day, or a couple of fat white juicy maggots.

Freddie kept his worms in a tin of damp moss in the shade at the back of the tent. Maggots were different, you had to be cunning to keep maggots which could climb out of any tin. Freddie bred maggots; he hung by their tails two dead pike in a tree, flies infested the putrid fish and maggots resulted. To harvest the maggots he held a jam jar under the open mouths of the pike and tapped the corpses with a stick, whereupon the maggots fell into the jar.

He sat beside the lake one afternoon having baited his hook with a worm of good size. He always felt sorry for worms when he put them on the hook but it had to be done. Now the worm had been cast out into the lake under a red-topped cork float. Freddie watched the float and when it bobbed upon the water he struck and eased the trout towards his landing net. Five fish were landed in this manner. He thought 'I'd better make it half-a-dozen and then go in for tea'.

He cast out again with two maggots on the hook, sat down and watched. This time the float did not bob upon the water but went straight down and disappeared. The line ran off the reel, the rod bent into a fighting arc as Freddie set his feet, arched his back and fought the underwater monster. After a while he saw he had an eel, a monstrous eel, fully a yard long.

The eel made a slimy mess of his net and wound his tackle into a slippery jumble. He hit the eel on the head with his priest, an iron field gate latch, and looked for the hook. The nylon went down deep into the eel's gullet where the hook could not be seen even though it was of a good size. Despairing of recovering the hook Freddie cut the nylon just inside the eel's mouth. He then dropped the creature into a plastic bag and tied the neck with string.

His uncle was delighted to have the five plump trout but declined to accept the eel which they laid out on the grass and measured: it was fully 3 ft and 2 inches in length, a fat, squirming succulent treat for any eel fancier.

After a moments thought his uncle said "Give it to the cowman, Alf, he comes from the East End in London. Up there they all eat eels".

Alf was Freddie's friend. They made catapults together from ash branches in the copse and hunted rats by the henhouses with Bonkers, Alf's terrier. The cowman accepted the eel, he would have it for supper that night. They parted in the evening light, the eel still squirming in the bag.

Freddie went to bed as usual but in the night he awoke with a dreadful thought 'the large hook was still in the eel, Alf didn't know, he would swallow the hook and surely die'.

Next morning the cowman was missing from the cowshed which was being washed down by his uncle. "Where's Alf?" asked Freddie, "is he dead?" "Oh no," replied his uncle, "Why should he be dead? He's got a tin-lined stomach, a fat eel doesn't trouble his gut. He sent you this hook and advised you sharpen up the point a bit as eels have leathery stomachs".

The Empty House above the River

THE FIRST PERSONS TO occupy Moorhayes in 1818 arrived on foot and horseback, with their farming stock and furniture on three carts. Two children rode on the carts because they wore no shoes, and although the September ground was not yet cold it was rough with granite chippings. The carts were laden with all the family's domestic possessions as well as coops of hens; the ducks and geese travelled silently in the darkness of confining sacks. A milk cow was roped to the back of the second cart and the procession was trailed by two black and white collie dogs who sometimes left the cavalcade to follow the farmer on the horse. The dogs trotted rapidly, short-stepped with heads low, swinging from one side to the other of the hedge-less stony track which rose from the valley to the moorland farm above the river.

The house had been completed by the estate three weeks before and the woman's husband had already driven the flock of ninety-three ewes from their previous farm near Moreton to the two hundred and forty three acres at Little

Moorhayes which they were now to occupy. Little enough land of poor quality to support the sheep, but there were common grazing rights. The farmer drank and his shiftless ways were the reason for the move from the comparative comfort of lowland Moreton to the higher land of Moorhayes. The woman had long ceased to fight against her lot; better to have a farm than none at all and with a cow and hens she could fill the bellies of the children.

The house faced north east on a slope overlooking the river, being protected from the south west gales by a hill to the rear. The walls were of granite, the joists of pine rough hewn from the forest, and elm had been used for the bedroom floorboards which creaked beneath their feet. It was a relief to the farmer and his wife that the roof had the permanence of slate, it would last their time at least, though lacking the warmth of thatch. The black cast iron stove in the single living room would become the heart of the house, but despite the stove there was no doubt that the two bedrooms would be desperately cold in winter, for Moorhayes was 1200 ft above the sea. The woman shivered as she thought of the coming months. She no longer complained at the trials of life and without a doubt was better off than the Frenchies confined in the dripping walls of the new prison at Princetown. Poor men, Bonaparte had brought them little luck or comfort, just the snows of Russia, the fleas of Spain and at times no pay for wine, little food, and not much leather for boots.

The family settled in, the years passed, warm summers were followed by damp winters of rain, snow, frost and drifting mists. No fat came off the land. Lambs were born at less than one a ewe and the time came when the farmer could not pay for lowland winter keep. He would sell up and go, having heard there was an ostler's job at The White Hart in Moretonhampstead.

Other families followed without success. The last to leave did so after standing a rough stone cross at the head of the river pool below the house; their daughter of five years of age had been found drowned in the water by the farmer's wife. The man stamped down the final sods around the base of the stone, turned and spat on the land which had defied his labour.

Because rent-paying tenants could not be found for the unsuccessful farm the house slowly decayed. "There's no point in maintenance," the bailiff said. Roof slates slipped and plaster ceilings fell, heavy from the rain which soaked down from the faulty roof.

The first non-paying tenant, other than a barn owl, spiders and mice, was a jackdaw which came in March with his grey-headed mate. He had recently been the occupier of a disused chimney at Great Moorhayes, but this had been wired over and a new nesting site had to be found. The jackdaws dropped sticks down the chimney until they lodged to create a platform. On this they built their nest of leaves, heather and bent grasses, lining the bowl with wool plucked from the backs of sheep and the thorns of blackthorn bushes against which the ewes rubbed to relieve the itch of lice. For many years their descendants returned to the chimney, each season bringing an increase in the pile of sticks which sheltered woodlice and became the winter retreat of mice which built their own nests inside the jackdaws' debris. Moorland ponies grazed up to the windows and sheep and cattle sheltered from the driving winds behind the walls of the roofless barn. Fishermen on the river looked up at the gaunt old house and wondered what was hidden behind the vacant stare of the dark windows. An aura of mystery enveloped the place, and those who climbed inside through a window to shelter from a storm became uncomfortable: they listened to the rain upon the roof, the patter of drips upon the ceiling and the sighs of cold winds under the creaking, swinging door: they did not linger when the rain had passed.

In the 1950s an ex-U.S. army jeep drew up beside the stone wall surrounding the Moorhayes yard. A young man with shoulder length fair hair swung down his legs on the near side, but his companion, a girl in her twenties, looked at the house whilst remaining seated in the open rusty vehicle. "Come on Sue," he called, "you might as well see where we're going to live this summer". The girl looked. It was, as he said when he had returned to her in London after his inspection a week ago, the most wonderful place, though how she would cope in the house she really did not know. She considered him as he pulled a heavy green tarpaulin out of the back of the jeep. It didn't matter what he did she'd go with him. "Might be different," she thought, "if we were married and certainly this was no place to live in the winter". She looked down the hill stretching below the house to the river winding through the valley. In June, July and August it would be warm and carefree, she would do as she liked whilst he painted his pictures.

The man had seen the place whilst walking on the moor and his enquiries had led him to the agent of the estate who was pleased to accept £100 as rent for three months. "The floors are not much good but the water from the spring is pure and I'll lend you a canvas sheet for the roof". 'Some people do the craziest things,' he thought, but the young man looked a decent sort of chap even if he was one of those artistic fellows. Perhaps if it worked out satisfactorily in the three months he might do the old house up a bit, put on a new roof, fit replacement windows and let the place regularly for a higher sum in the summer season.

The couple swept out the house, installed camp beds upstairs and a bottled gas cooker in the kitchen. At times, whilst he painted for his coming November exhibition in London, the girl walked the three miles to the Post Office to shop. She carried a rucksack on her back and enjoyed discovering the history of the place from the postmistress. "Back along it were a real boody (beauty) place," the old woman told her, "but it weren't never a lucky 'ouse. Forty year ago there were a couple there an' I'd goo along an' 'elp 'er out from time to time, but then 'er li'l maid were drowned. I 'elped 'er pull un out, poor li'l thing, 'er bein' so small. They lef' after that, 'and't no 'eart for the place I reckon". The old woman moved to shut the door because it was time to close for the afternoon. "mus' be movin' on m'dear. Us be goin' to Moreton to see me daughter's babe".

The girl walked back to the house, following the track which wound through the rough grass and heather. It was sad that so beautiful a place had been the scene of penury and misfortune, perhaps it should never have been built for work but as the fishing lodge of some gentleman of means. She dumped the rucksack on the kitchen floor before going out to search for Harry. She found him seated on a rock painting a picture of three ponies by a river pool. "Sue, shall we come back next year? I've finished seven pictures and, if they sell well and I do a few more this winter in Switzerland, we could afford to come again. How about it?" They drove away a week later in the old jeep leaving behind the stove, tinned foods, the beds and sleeping bags. The agent said they could come back in the spring or any other time they liked.

Four months later in January, Westerfield (Westy to his mates in Dartmoor prison) sighed with relief as the group of four prisoners with two warders passed out of the prison onto the road. Out here he could stretch his eyes, look at the sky, be free of the smell of the nick. For a few hours whilst working on the farm he would pretend he was back on the Yorkshire moors which were his home. It was his own fault that he was here, he had to admit it, but also bad luck and due to his excitable nature. He had been poaching pheasants whilst out of work, a keeper had surprised him and he had fired his gun in the air to stop the man chasing him through the woods. Returning to his van by a circuitous route he had found the police waiting for him, and here he was.

Westy looked about and up at the January sky; it would snow, he decided, the grey stones and walls would be covered and he could then imagine himself elsewhere. The group walked over green fields dotted with tufts of reeds where the water hung about in shallow pools. Reaching a hut one of the warders unlocked the door with a key which he pulled from his pocket at the end of a chain. Two mallets were brought out, with two iron bars to make holes in the ground. Their task was to erect a line of fence posts and then wire them to contain the cattle of the prison farm. One man of a pair made the hole with the bar and the other hammered in the post, the line being kept straight by the eye of a warder at either end. Westy spat on his hands, brought down the iron bar with force and to his satisfaction it sank to half its length in the waterlogged ground. Too soft by far he thought as his mate drove in the post. Still, if they wanted a fence here they could have a fence here, it really didn't matter to him. He looked about, considering his position, the confining prison to his left and on the right the clean, far-flung freedom of the moor. Just for a day or two of space he would make a break, it was a 'spur of the moment' decision. He made another hole, put down the bar, and, taking up a fence post, called the nearer warder over whilst pointing into the hole which was rapidly filling with water. The screw looked into the hole as Westy rammed down the post, causing a fountain of watery mud to burst up into the bent-over face of the man. The warder swore, searched for his handkerchief, wiped his face, his eyes and hair and turned to Westy—but Westerfield had gone.

There was not much they could do late on that January afternoon, for a swirling mist came down and soon the night closed in. The police blocked the roads leading off the moor and inspected all cars leaving the area. Snow fell in the dark hours and the higher roads became impassable. They didn't think he had gone far but warned the Yorkshire police in case he had got away, and telephoned a warning to the people in the local moorland houses.

Westy ran on in the falling dusk. He had little idea of the direction to take but wanted to find a stream to follow. The flow would lead him down to a river and if he followed this not only would it lead him off the moor but almost certainly to a farm with a barn where he could sleep. The donkey jacket he was wearing was warm, but not warm enough for January at 1500 ft above the sea. He must go down or he would freeze. He came to a leat from which he drank briefly and then ran on downhill. Crossing a road he came at last to a river. There was ice along the edges and the banks were rough, causing him to stumble, but he continued on, breathing in rasping gasps. The snow stopped for a while, the moon came out, the going improved as the river ran through upland fields white with snow. Westy's heart was pounding, he knew he must stop soon in shelter for in his present state he would lose heat rapidly and might die of exposure before the night was out.

He looked across the moonlit white expanse to a dark area of trees where there appeared to be a cattle shed. Westy climbed over the Moorhayes wall beside the house with care. He circled the property. It seemed to be derelict, and yet not quite for there were empty food tins at the back. Coming closer he threw a pebble against a window and then another at the door, they rattled, but no dog barked. He pushed at the door which dragged open over the stone slabs of the floor and entered, treading on moonbeams which shone through a window onto the floor and illuminated the room to his right. The living room was large with a central scrubbed pine table, at either end of which was placed a log seat. He sat down, his arms on the table and with his head on his hands rested whilst his heart calmed. Later he rose to climb the stairs which creaked under the pressure of his boots. Finding two camp beds with sleeping bags in plastic sacks Westy lay down, covered himself and fell asleep.

For a moment on waking he was lost, no noise, no smell, no shouts or grating keys, no food either, he thought as realization of his isolation came to him. He stood up, keeping back from the window to look out through the dirty glass, then swung around, went out of the door to enter the other bedroom from which he carried out a second inspection of the land. More snow had fallen in the night to cover his footprints and no road or track could be seen. The house was as an oasis in the desert or a single small island in the centre of a lake. He looked again; there below him was the dark ribbon of the river running through the valley like a black snake. Behind the house the snowy hills stretched up and away, surmounted in places by isolated grey rocks from which the wind had swept the snow, a few sheep huddled behind a wall, a buzzard wheeled mewing in the sky, the sound cutting through the silence. Westerfield relaxed, it was like his Yorkshire moors. Tension receded, his brain ceased to hammer urgent thoughts inside his skull, two or three days here and when they come for me I'll go back inside a better man. He went downstairs to search the place and finding tinned food ate ravenously, pressing corned beef into his mouth spoonful upon spoonful. He found the spring behind the house: jutting out of a bank an iron pipe carried the even flow of water into the granite trough from which he filled a jug to carry back to the house. He remained inside for the rest of that day.

After four days it came to him that he could be there for weeks if the weather didn't break. The only sign of activity had been a single distant shepherd on a pony without dogs, he supposed the snow was too deep for the collies' legs. He was not badly off he thought, for the chimney, cleared of sticks, drew well at night when he lit a fire, having covered the window with a plastic sheet but he must have food for the tinned stock had been consumed and his energy and coherence of thought were reducing. If he left the place to search for a farmhouse from which to steal, his thefts would be noticed and the search, concentrated on the area, would find him. He looked morosely out of the window at a black spot on a wall one hundred yards away, it was a bird, a raven. The croaks of the bird reached him and with each call the bird leaned forward to emit the sound. Later it dropped out of sight behind the wall. Taking a knife Westerfield trudged over the bare snow to the shelter of the stones along which he crept to the dead sheep on which the bird had been feeding. Swaying, he pulled at the back leg but found the animal was frozen solid. He tried to pick it up but the weight and the clinging snow were too much for him. Westerfield knelt down, slit through the wool and skin to cut off the two back legs which he carried away to the house.

He boiled the meat and ate, cutting strips from the bone with the knife, tipping back his head and dropping them into his open mouth. The half raw meat distended him, he belched, then pressed his swollen belly with his hands. Rising, the mirror on the wall caught his eye. "Cor, stone the crows. That can't be me" he whispered at the apparition in the glass. Sunken eyes, a bearded dirty face topped by wild unkempt hair stared back at him. Westerfield sank back on the log by the table, put his face in his hands and cried.

More days passed, his body weakened, trembled and chilled. The mind became an indecisive whirl of thoughts and memories flitted through his skull as he sat, round shouldered, at the table. The police search found him when the snow melted. "A babbling ruin of a man," a warder told his wife later that evening in the comfort of his house. "Kept on about open places, and tried to run off when we reached the nick. Poor sod fell over. Better off inside, I say".

In London the artist and Sue read the account of the prisoner's arrest in the national press. "How horrible to think of that dirty man using all our things, perhaps my sleeping bag and our cups and plates". She felt violated; it was disgusting; she would not return.

The house relapsed into total disuse and they nailed up the door. When I last climbed to shelter from the rain whilst fishing, the sadness of the place pressed upon me and I left as soon as the rainstorm passed. Walking down the hill I felt the pressure of the dark eyes of the house on my back, staring from glassless window sockets.

The Heron and the
One-eyed Pilot

SOON AFTER DAWN Craak the heron flew a meandering course up the river valley on wide grey wings. His body fell a foot between beats and then a stroke wafted him up. Due to the lazy motion no wind whistled through Craak's flight pinions and his feet trailed behind at the end of the long legs tacked on, as it were, by his wife before he left the nest at dawn that April morning to fish and forage for their three scrawny youngsters. His relaxed appearance was deceptive for little escaped his yellow eyes. When hunting frogs, fish, young birds and other creatures in the fields, ditches and streams he lived by deception, stealth and the speed of his powerful stabbing beak.

April for Craak was a hard time. His youngsters daily grew larger, more raucous, with demanding appetites as they urged him to regurgitate the food he carried in his crop. There were not, as yet, many young rabbits about and the froglets were still at the tadpole stage. The supply of young birds was increasing but the plenteousness of May had not been reached. Wild trout of the rivers still inhabited the deeper pools for few flies hatched to bring them to the surface. But the heron could be assured of one good gathering of fish each day at the trout fishery at the head of the valley. He had to arrive in time to fill himself before the human opened the door of the mill house beside the trout pools. He flew on, rose up over a hill and there below him were five pools connected to the stream by a channel from which hatches fed them water. The trout farm and fishery was served on one side by a winding country lane and on the other side, some way from the mill house, a spinney reached almost to the water's edge and willow trees drooped their pale yellow branches to the grass. The heron set his wings to glide down to the pond furthest from the house. He alighted on the grass strip dividing the water from the spinney, settled his wings, looked about and stalked slowly to the edge of the pool.

Craak entered the pool with care, his head craning forward. In the water he became still and waited until a trout approached. His neck extended, the beak stabbed down and out came the fish, twisting in the gripping beak. Two more followed, of which the final fish was large enough to cause him to retreat onto the grass to batter the body with his beak, swallow the trout head first then jump into the air to fly home to the nest. The young ones greeted him with screams and croaks, extending their bills upwards to show the yellow throat. Craak regurgitated a slimy mess of fish onto the platform of sticks, then his mate picked over the trout whilst he stood morosely, head hunched into his shoulders.

Before the establishment of the trout farm the mill had been used to grind the corn of the small farms of the valley for many generations. During the Second World War the final miller had viewed from the top of the tower the red glow in the sky over Plymouth to the south. The structure of the building had been shaken by the distant explosions of bombs rained down on the town by Hitler's aeroplanes. He had watched the burning glow change to a pall of smoke as the guns fell silent and then, climbing down the wooden ladder he had set the mill stone revolving to grind the corn and earn his living.

Towards the end of the war the mill fell into disuse, grain being ground by modern machines owned by large companies remote from water-powered paddle wheels. The buildings and ponds were put up for sale. Two years after the cessation of hostilities a man appeared at the mill in a worn old car. He was not upset at the sight of the rotten wood of the paddle wheel and his eyes lit with satisfaction at the warm dryness of the interior of the building. He satisfied himself that there flowed clear and ample water in the leat. The man purchased the property and roughly converting the old mill lived inside by himself whilst he cleaned the ponds and channels to establish a trout farm and fishery.

The purchaser had come from the city to rebuild his physical and mental health. There was no need to ask the reason, for one did one's best to hide dismay at the sight of the skin stretched in tight whiteness over the left side of his face, the stumpy left ear and the patch over a sightless eye. He had been a fighter pilot burned out of the cockpit of his Spitfire over France in 1944. After the war the city rejected him in embarrassment and he had come to rebuild himself in the company of country people who would grow used to him. A trout farm had seemed a good idea and he installed himself in the mill, building a stone fireplace in the ground floor room where he could sit by a wood fire in a winged chair when winter froze outside. A photograph of his Spitfire hung on one wall and an oil painting of a flight of greylag geese, outlined against the yellow orange of a sunset, was set above the mantelpiece. A monocular hung from a peg beside the fire alongside a bookcase. Birds seemed his main interest from the titles, also falconry, fishing and the sports cars of the pre-war era. He installed a bottled gas cooker below the window which overlooked the leat where kingfishers sat upon the stone sides of the water channel, diving in to emerge with tiny fish which they flicked to death upon the stone and then swallowed. The stubby blue bodies of the kingfishers delighted him.

A wooden ladder led up to his bedroom where he made and placed an oaken cot, softening the base with a hair mattress. The pilot covered himself at night with grey army blankets, and with the passing of the months, and the

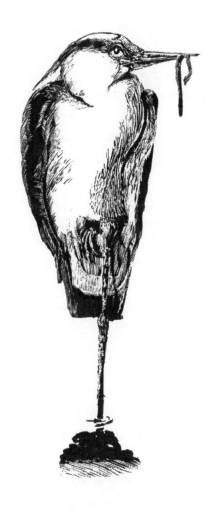

quietness of the nights, the angry flames ceased to waken him and his hands no longer clawed at the Perspex canopy above his head. He became tranquil and the fire was cooled by the balm of flowing water channelled in his leats and held within the ponds. He could not yet say that the trout farm paid, but he reaped the benefit of life renewed.

The pilot was not meticulous in his ways upon the farm but by the end of April even he noticed a reduction in the number of trout held in the pond beside the spinney. The widespread toes of Craak left footprints in the mud and even the pilot, who wished to be at peace with all, had to do something to stop the loss. He rose before dawn to watch the pool from the mill tower, peering out through the cobwebbed glass of the little window high above the ground. He saw Craak drop on widespread wings, fold them down and stalk towards the pool. He could not bring himself to shoot the bird but he had heard that wires stretched between the trees would stop a heron landing. Later, the pilot placed three tightly drawn wires twelve feet above the ground between the willows. He meant to tie strips of cloth to the wires to warn off the bird, but as he was about to do so a visitor arrived and he forgot about the cloth.

That night the pilot went to bed as usual and, as was his practice, Craak flew to the pond at first light. A wire caught his left wing as he descended, breaking the bone above the elbow in the section where the secondary flight feathers grow. He tumbled to earth with a harsh scream, jumped towards the sky to take off, but beat as he could with the one sound wing he could not rise from the ground. Craak then hid in a corner under a bush where the pilot found him later in the morning when feeding trout, having forgotten all about the wires. Yesterday he was filled with ill thoughts toward the heron but today he was gripped with guilty concern on seeing the suffering bird. He smothered

the heron's bill with a blanket, took the bird inside to trim off the flight feathers and set the wing which he bound against the heron's body. The bird would moult in time, growing new feathers to give him flight. As a temporary measure he placed the heron in the hut where he stored the trout pellets whilst he erected a netting fence enclosing the hut, several square yards of rough grass, and a disused trout rearing pond. He then opened the door of the hut, placed two flapping fish upon the grass and retreated into the mill to watch.

Craak had recovered himself inside the hut, he was hungry, not having eaten since the previous evening when, after feeding the young, he had made do with a water vole which he had swallowed whole after puncturing the skull with his beak. He peered out of the door at the trout which twitched on the grass. Stepping down from the hut in an awkward lopsided manner towards the fish his beak flashed out, gripped a trout, swallowed the first and then the second. Craak looked about, tried to jump the wire, failed and retreated inside the hut from which he did not again emerge. At dusk the pilot looked through the door to see him roosting on one leg on a sack of fish pellets, the other foot being drawn up to the bandage strapping his wing to his body.

In time the heron became tame, causing the pilot to remove the wire netting surrounding the hut, whereupon the bird fed himself, standing up to his knees in the water to stab at passing fish. He kept the farm free of rats, waiting motionless as a wooden post beside their paths to catch them as they scuttled from one building to another. He ate the chicks of moorhens; he ate frogs, mice, and the elvers which migrated up the streams to grow in the ponds before returning to the sea and their journey to the Sargasso Sea to breed in the

South Atlantic. He picked the sunning lizards off the stones at the base of the mill, and in time, he took trout from the pilot's hand. But always the pilot watched the stabbing beak, fearful of his sole remaining eye, and he wore a thick leather glove when offering a fish.

The strangeness of the pilot's ways caused gossip in the pub and cottages. "He'm strange, him from upalong the mill. Touched by th' war ee be I 'low. Eee got a girt bird, a 'eron which do foller 'im about". On the whole the village liked the pilot and, whilst a one-eyed flyer and a one-winged bird did not fall readily into the rural scene, they were prepared to defend his eccentricities to foreigners, wrapping a cloak of mystery around the man. He took to visiting the public house in the quiet of the morning, and at times the bird followed him down the lane. At the pub Craak waited in a dark corner, watched by the landlord, the pilot and the landlord's terrified cat which hid behind the R.N. Lifeboat collecting box on the bar. These visits were highlighted by an event which shook even the landlord who had spent most of his life as a sailor at sea in foreign parts where he had seen the wonders of the world. "True as I'm standin' 'ere," vouched the ex-sailor, "'ee made a sudden movement to touch the bird's bad wing an' th' varmint poked 'im in th' face. The pilot's head jerked back and his hand flew to his eye". The landlord drank from his pewter jar, enjoying the tension as his customers waited. "That pilot walked to the window, pulled off the patch and held it up to the light to inspect a bullet-sized hole in the centre. 'ee replaced the patch, pulling the elastic over 'is head. All 'ee said were "Shaky to do that, might have bought it in the other blinker". Then 'ee went orf 'ome, the bird follerin 'im, and 'ee were cool as a cucumber".

The Ivy Berry Salmon Fly

TO THE SALMON FLYFISHER the winter months are a long drawn out period of waiting for the warm waters and breezes of spring. Charlie could imagine the rain storm which would raise the water level and excite salmon to move up the river from pool to pool, and he could feel the fly line tighten as one took his fly. But it was all in his mind; so long to wait. He put down the silks, tinsels and bucktail on his fly dressing bench, switched off the lamp and went downstairs.

By the fire in the sitting room he shared with his college friend, Ted, he picked up Izaak Walton's *The Compleat Angler* and idly turned the pages until he came to The Fourth Day, and Izaak's seventeenth century dissertation on salmon. Surely there would be something he could learn from that angling sage: there it was, ivy berries! He read on: 'And now I shall tell you that which may be called a secret. I have been a-fishing with old Oliver Henley, now with God, a noted fisher for Trout and Salmon...observed by others and myself to catch more fish than I or any other body...especially Salmons'. Charlie read that Oliver's worms were kept in a box where they became anointed with a drop, or two or three, of the oil of ivy berries, and that the ivy-berried worms...'had incorporated a kind of smell that was irresistibly attractive, enough to force any fish within the smell of them to bite'.

Charlie thought of Devon where he fished a 'fly-only' water. The worm was not allowed, in fact if an angler was caught with one on his hook he would be thrown off the river and ostracised. The trout fishers had a two-hook-in-line fly called the Worm Fly which did not look like anything natural he had seen. No. The trout Worm Fly would be no use at all, and its weak hooks would not hold a salmon, but it was still acknowledged as a fly.

He decided to dress his own worm fly, one specially designed for salmon and place this in a little box with a few drops of oil of ivy berries and try it out next May. A rubber tube for the body would not do, for rubber would not absorb the ivy oil, he must use a natural material of a red/brown colour. Red would be helpful in itself for fish see the red end of the spectrum better than the blue end. He pulled out of his materials box a deer tail that had been dyed red and was thus the colour of an enticing worm.

Charlie sat at his fly-tying bench and tightened the vice on to the bend of a No. 1/0 single barbless hook and then wound side-by-side turns of brown silk down the shank from eye to bend. Taking the longest hairs from the tail end of the bucktail he laid them along the shank of the hook and then ribbed them with fine copper wire to look like the segments of a worm's body. Finally at the start of the bend he tied in a thin strip of bucktail skin to make the fly three inches in length. All that remained was to dap a spot of red varnish on the head of the fly to secure the silk wrapping.

"Ted," he called. "We are going to collect ivy berries". Having found a tree where the ivy had not been stripped of berries by the woodpigeons, they crushed the berries, putting them in a small tin which enclosed the oil and the fly, together with a spare fly Charlie had dressed in case of need.

May, and the Whitsun week-end when the fly would be tried, was a long time coming. Their college was in Gloucestershire and early on the Whit Friday morning they packed the car with a tent, Gaz cooker, kettle, frying pan, sleeping bags, wine and their fishing tackle. They arrived in Devon and set up camp by the river which ran low and clear. The water being too low for salmon they fished for trout which they cooked and ate by an open fire on the river bank as the sun went down and rain clouds gathered over the western hills.

The rain came after midnight, heavy drops fell on the tent from overhead trees and soon water crept under their groundsheet and then reached the sleeping men. Next morning they packed up their gear and migrated to The Pine Tree Inn two miles down the river which had risen and now ran at an inviting height. The water, too, was tinted a whisky shade which was too opaque for a fly but just right for the worm. They assembled the three sections of the 12 ft salmon fly rod, ran a sink-tip line up through the guides and knotted on a 12 lb, 9 ft nylon leader to the point of which they tied the worm fly from which the ivy oil dripped.

Making their way to Church Pool in the rain, Charlie cast the fly in at the head, the fly was swept around to hang high in the water downstream of his position—nothing. Withdrawing the fly Charlie nipped a bead of tungsten putty on to the head of the fly and cast again. The fly sank at once, then came round slowly, trundling over the bedstones of the river and a salmon took. Ted netted the fish, removed the hook and returned the salmon to the river. The second salmon, a 5 lb grilse, they kept as a gift for the landlady of their lodgings.

The third, fourth and fifth fish were also returned by which time the ever-popular fly, gnashed by many teeth, was in tatters and they had become bored with success.

Whilst knotting on the spare fly from the ivy oil box there was a clap of thunder and a voice disturbed them. They turned to find a tweedy ancient leaning over their shoulders peering at the fly. In a windswept voice the ancient said "Izaak told me more than once I could have saved myself much toil in digging up worms if I learned to dress flies. By the way, my name is Henley, Oliver Henley". Turning away, he walked downstream and was lost to sight in a low drifting rain cloud.

The Peal Fisher's Return?*

PREPARATIONS FOR RIVER sea trout fishing at night take place in the afternoon at home. I prepare two rods: one for fishing wet fly or lure beneath the water surface, the other for drawing a wake-producing floating fly across the river surface.

Then, after supper, I drive across Dartmoor to our stretch of river which is near the site of an old abbey, now restored.

Arriving at the river in waist waders, the sub-surface fly and leader are put to soak in the water whilst I sit on the bank and wait for the light to fade. It is fatal to start fishing before it is fully dark, if you do the fish will be scared by the flash of the fly line and success will be delayed.

Waiting for full dark has its rewards: you may hear a bitch otter squeak to call her cubs across the water. Certainly tawny owls will hoot, and a heron may fly up the river at dusk. Can herons fish in the dark? I do not know, but they arrive at dusk to land on the river bank. Whilst I sit I note

*This is not a story, it is an account. (Peal is the Devon name for a sea trout.)

128

where peal jump clear of the water to bash down and send waves rippling to the banks. I look over my shoulder nervously from time to time, for who is not startled by the snuffle of a badger or the squeal of a rabbit caught by a stoat? Of people there are none.

When I hook, play and net a sea trout I wade ashore, kneel down, hold a torch in my teeth and attend to the fish which is bathed in a pool of light. All around is the enveloping night and you are at the mercy of anything or anyone creeping up on you from the black beyond. Consequently I sometimes flash the torch to penetrate the surrounding gloom but have never seen a soul. And then one night I did.

I was wading thigh-deep with the line drifting slowly across the river. By chance I turned towards the bank and there, fifteen yards away, illuminated by a waning moon, faintly pink in colour, stood the figure of a man who watched me fish. I called "What do you want. Who are you?" There was no response, he just stood there and watched me. For half-a-minute I had to attend to my line or the fly would have become hooked on the river bed. Turning again I saw that the figure had moved away a little. He still regarded me and glowed, but faintly. I called again "Who are you. Are you from the cottage?" There was no reply. The figure moved away down the riverside path, the pink glow died and then there was nothing.

I climbed out of the river, put down my rod and searched the path in the direction in which the figure had faded. Nobody was revealed. Little fear of the unknown enveloped me as I searched towards the abbey. Thinking back as I drove home I was drawn warmly to the figure for he had the gift of silence, a welcome attribute in any peal angling companion, perhaps he had fished the river as a monk in centuries gone by.

My fishing friends are sceptical. They say "Charles should take more water with it", but I am not dissuaded for I have been backed-up by a friend who said "You know that little field we have to cross on our way to the river, the one which used to belong to the abbey. Well, one evening I was waiting to fish in the failing evening light and I saw a figure start to cross the field. When it reached the centre it faded away".

The Pheromone Fly

THEY SAT ON THE ROCKS with the salmon close to them on the grass. It was a fine silver fish of fifteen pounds. They should have been happy but he was sour and he would stay sour, thought Andrew, even if she stopped needling him. She should stop needling him. She knows he knows she despises him and that I know too. There are only the three of us and he has been shamed. She ought to stop. She ought not to reduce him further. Perhaps she would cease when she became cold which would be soon as she was wet and her clothes dripped water.

Andrew pulled a flask from his pocket and offered it to her. She took a pull holding the silver container in long fingers with manicured nails. The nails were long as well as the fingers which were dead white with cold. Even when wet and cold she was beautiful. Tall, decisive and beautiful. She had intimated to the man that he was not good enough for her. She'd done it and he knew. She swallowed the whisky, shuddered and handed the flask back to Andrew who passed it on to James. He swallowed some whisky. "It's a good fish"— he tipped the flask again—"here's to mine, when it comes".

131

Now, he no longer wanted a salmon, just to go back to his house in London and forget that he had brought her to Devon. He didn't really know her and now regretted his action. Somehow she had made him bring her. He was overweight, soft, and had just shown that he lacked guts. He had plenty of money, was good at driving his expensive car, buying clothes, and ordering food and wine in restaurants. She looked desirable beside him in the car, but he wished he hadn't brought her. She had come because she was husband hunting but, from half an hour ago, she also wished she had stayed in London.

He had hooked the salmon whilst casting in a stylish manner, and had played the fish from the bank with the rod arched high whilst Andrew waited with the net, up to his thighs in the swift current of the river. The salmon had bolted downstream past Andrew where James could not follow because of a bankside tree. He had stood there with the line snaking off the reel, refusing to jump in to follow the fish and trust to luck not to lose his footing and be washed away. He lacked the stomach for the risk. Andrew had wrenched the rod from him, jumped in and girl had slid down the bank into the river.

"Give me the rod".

"You want to watch the holes or you'll be swept away".

"Give it to me".

He had followed her. She floundered up to her waist in and out of the rocks, tripping and splashing and swearing and soaked. Sometimes the tip of the fly rod was in the water when she lost her balance, but she got there. Andrew netted the salmon, astonished at her courage.

Later, Andrew, a professional angler, returned them to their hotel and then went on to his batchelor cottage on the moor. She bathed in the hotel, dressed for dinner, and descended to James in the bar. Men eyed her; she them. James' eyes slid by her.

The next day she played golf with James, without interest in him or the game. Her mind strayed back to Andrew in his old boots and jacket. His brown face, large hands, and the neck which became a white ring where he had undone his collar to cool himself after landing the salmon.

On the third day they went salmon fishing again, Andrew calling for them at the hotel after breakfast. James sat in the front seat of the car. She sat behind, studying Andrew. 'He's steady and tough. I could go for him' and other traces of thoughts flickered through her mind. Andrew drove on. Her presence disturbed him and he glanced in the mirror. She would be a complication after the first joys, and would be unlikely to fit his way of life. It would be a stupid thing to do. He decided to conduct the day's fishing on a formal basis and then have no more to do with them. It was James' problem to return her to London.

He pulled the car off the road into the track leading to the river, switched off and climbed out. They put up the rods and walked to the river. James set off upstream, glad to be alone. She went downstream through the woods and Andrew remained where he was, sitting on the rocks where they had laid the salmon two days before. He followed James up the river and spent two hours pointing out salmon lies. They all had lunch by the rocks, after which she set off up the river. In a while Andrew followed her. He was undecided and irritated at this disruption of his world. Yet, she excited him.

The day was warm and he found her sitting on the grass with her back to a tree tying on a feathered salmon fly. She was making a mess of it. He sat down nearby on the grass, she brought the fly and nylon to him and leaned over to watch him tie the knot. Her blouse was loose, and she stayed, leaning over. Andrew ignored the invitation, tightened the knot, bit off the end of nylon, spat it out, then handed her the fly. Taking it, her pink tongue flicked out, slicking down the feathers. He rose and she straightened, angry at the rejection. He felt disappointed with himself and yet relieved. Anyway, he thought, the restlessness will pass—let's go and catch a salmon. Neither of them caught a fish that day. There was tension in the car on the way back to the hotel. Andrew, driving, regretted his caution and lost opportunity—perhaps he would follow her to London.

From the hotel the girl took a taxi to the station, catching a train to town. She was restless, her problem unresolved. Alighting at Paddington she took the tube to her mother's flat. A small boy ran to her.

"Mummy, mummy did you find a daddy for me?"

She picked him up to explain that daddies were not easily caught in Devon. She had found one but it might be a few days before he arrived.

In his cottage Andrew lay alone that night thinking of a pink tongue and a pheromone-flavoured fly.

The Pool at Stoney Cross*

FOR SEVERAL YEARS I had seen a man by the river on my fishing visits. He rarely spoke so that for a long time I felt he disapproved of my presence or was secretive of his favourite fishing places but it was not so, he just liked to be alone.

"My wife says I am no good at earning a living as a solicitor," he told me one day when I knew him better. "But I don't care. I work four days a week and fish the other three, and if I can't fish I walk on the moor".

It would be difficult to describe his clothes, particularly their colour, as all were of a uniform grubbiness, in fact they were best likened to the coat of his brown and scruffy dog. They were well matched, the man and his small dog, for the animal followed the attitude of his master and showed little respect for any other dog regardless of their size. It may be that other dogs found him unsavoury and thus not to be

---

*On a hillside above the pool which I have named Stoney Cross is a derelict isolated farmhouse in which lived the family of the drowned child; the house was then abandoned. In past seasons, driven by sweeping rainstorms from the river I would climb the hillside, push open the creaking door which hung drunkenly on rusty hinges, and take shelter.

bitten with impunity. Most days the dog followed the solicitor along the river bank and enjoyed the fishing as much as his master, which was very much indeed. "I can't keep the blighter out of the river," the solicitor said, "as soon as I hook a fish he's in and after it". He stirred the woolly animal absent-mindedly with his foot, and scratched his own neck which was being bitten by the midges, and the dog yawned and scratched its hairless belly in sympathy. Sheep ticks were clearly attracted to the animal.

"Had any peal?" he asked me and I had to admit that I had not met with much success that season. "You should use a two-inch silver fly with a blue wing, three hooks in line and plenty of jungle cock on the cheeks," he advised. "Well, I must be on my way, see you by the heron pond one day". By this I knew he referred to the local reservoir, stocked with rainbow trout, an artificial place which he frequented but despised, saying it was stocked with plastic fish. The dog lifted his leg against a rock close to my foot, passed me with indifference and followed his master up the valley. They both blended so well with the heather, gorse and bushy scrub that within a few minutes I could no longer make them out.

I met him again two weeks before the end of the season.
I was carrying a salmon of about ten pounds but was altogether
in a gloomy state, having fallen over whilst netting the fish and
broken the tip of my rod, the only one I had, other than trout
rods. He heard the story, took in the situation and looked at
me wickedly. "River'll keep up well the next two weeks." I
nodded glumly. "Plenty of salmon about." The dog wagged its
tail with enthusiasm. "No second rod, you say." He rubbed it
in. The two or three miles of river we fished was ticket water
where anyone might go, and thus the activities of the solicitor
and myself were in friendly competition. One day he would be
carrying a fish when we met and the next it would be his turn
to conceal an envious glance. The situation of the broken rod
and my impecunious state, which precluded the purchase of
a replacement, obviously delighted him. "Rod repairs take a
long time," he said mischievously, "but I know a good man in
Poundsworthy. Make a proper job of it, perhaps not for this
season though". He named a rod repairer notorious in the local
community for the slowness of his work. "You might send it
up to Alnwick—Hardy's do a good job. Of course there's always
a bit of a delay."

My downcast state must have touched some chord of
memory—perhaps he had been in the same situation when
a younger man. He would tease me no more. Who knows,
one day he might be floating down the river with his boots
full, or have a fish stuck around a mid-stream rock and I
would pass by on the other side. A little insurance against
the future would do no harm and anyway, I think he had
decided he liked me. The dog moved closer with cocked ear.
Surely his master wasn't going to help the opposition, why
couldn't he stop this chatter and get on with the fishing?
Humans were so silly making these ridiculous noises

between themselves when there were miles of marvellous smells to be investigated up the river bank. Perhaps, delight of delights, a defunct and richly odorous mole or fitch to be rolled upon in smelly ecstasy. He ran a short way upstream to provide a lead and looked back hopefully. The solicitor glanced at the dog, realised that a salmon taking-time might be imminent with the river in such good ply and came to a decision. "Go up to my cottage on the hill, let yourself in by the key hanging behind the outhouse door and take the rod you'll find hanging by a nail near the fireplace. Don't look about too much, place is in a terrible state, haven't cleared up for weeks."

I let myself into one of the untidiest, most muddly, but happiest rooms I have entered. Of small size, the greater part of the space was taken up by a large pine table, a dresser, two or three wooden chairs and on all of these were the various items the man used to follow his lonely country pursuits, for his wife lived in their town flat, close to his practice. A large open chimney rose above a solid, rough granite fireplace in which was a heap of grey wood ash, no doubt last winter's accumulation. Old leather boots, fishing rods, neglected brass reels more than fifty years of age with the silk lines still upon them, line driers, nets, fly boxes— the place was a collectors' dream. "Don't look about" he had said. I couldn't help it, I was hushed and almost ceased to breathe for I had entered that man's inner life. How he had achieved this splendid disorder and, at the same time, supported himself in a modest way in a meticulous profession I really did not know.

I took down the rod. 'J. Somers & Son, Aberdeen,' stated the label on the cloth sleeve which had been green but was now grey with age. At home I examined the contents. A greenheart of twelve feet in length, the three sections being spliced. The small pocket inside the flap of the case held two leather thongs of about two feet each in length to bind the sections together. It was a lovely thing with an action so smooth that it was possible to imagine it part of oneself whilst laying out a line across the river. It would not be readily repaired these days. How good of him to trust me with this window into bygone fishing years and scenes.

That night the rain lashed against my bedroom window, a wonderful sound, prelude to many moorland salmon days. By morning the garden rainfall gauge, an inverted dustbin lid, was full. There could be no doubt, a visit to the river must be made.

High up the valley the solicitor walked upstream that afternoon. His salmon rod pointed back towards the woods from whose warm steamy cover he had emerged. He carried his rod butt first at the trail and in this way did not have to bother about it, for he could not dig the tip into the ground or a wall and snap if off. He could walk automatically, dream a bit, lose himself in country thoughts whilst observing unconsciously the river, a leaping fish, the buzzards, dippers and crows. He knew them all, their ways of movement and communication, the contented noises, the alarmed cry of the surprised crow, the curious magpie's chatter and the raucous scolding of the jay. Mostly he looked at the ground just in front of his boots to avoid the tripping rock and unsuspected hole. The muddy patches told their tale of other users of the path—the mink's narrow print with needle claws, the heron's three wide forward toes with one behind, were clear indication of his earlier search for frogs who also used the path. Infrequently these days he saw a track which gave the keenest pleasure—fat round forward toes, arranged fan-shaped before the plump central pad of the footprint of the otter. Solitary, like himself, a fisher as he was, sometimes playful like his dog, taking no heed for the future as he himself took little heed, and only one coat to worry about. The gentle river valley gave way to a harsher scene as his steps carried him higher on the moor: bog, heather, gorse and thorn replaced oak, sycamore and bracken. He was making for the Stone Cross pool, or Stoney, as he called this salmon holding water. A lonely place frequented by curlews, moorland ponies and the Galloway cattle who came to the river to drink. A heron jumped into the air with sweeping grey wings uttering a single harsh "Craak". This was a welcome sight for the heron fished alone and no other angler would be near. The solicitor sat on a rock on the bank, with his back to a roughly hewn stone cross, and watched the water rushing by between the boulders. A strong wind blew upstream creating great waves in the pool as it fought the current—a brave sight to stir the heart of any salmon man. A fish leaped above the large central rock in the tail of the pool. "He's been in the river a long time", muttered the solicitor who had seen the black flanks of the fish. He sat on for a while longer, pulled a tin of beer from his pocket and two pork pies, one of which he gave to the dog. Time enough to catch the fish before the light gave out. He didn't doubt the fate of the salmon for they always took his fly when in that lie with the water as it was. There might even be a second fish and, if it all took a little longer than he anticipated, the night and darkness held no fear. He would wait a while and carry the fish home by the light of the moon which would shine through the scudding clouds.

The beer had made him sleepy, his eyelids drooped and in time his chin fell forward on his chest. The dog moved closer, curled its back against his master's thigh, twitched and likewise fell asleep. As he slept his master dreamed of a girl child who stood beside the water and asked him not to kill the salmon of the pool. He had no fear but when he woke he looked uneasily about and the dog too seemed upset, whined and looked intently at the black and swirling river.

I called at his cottage that evening to thank him for the loan of the rod. He had a fire going, some whisky out to soothe himself, and we sat for a while by the flickering firelight. "Did you get a fish this afternoon?" I asked as he sat and smoked his pipe. "To tell the truth" he replied, "I didn't fish. I walked to Stoney Cross but it seemed a bit cold and I felt uneasy and thought perhaps a Dartmoor prisoner was on the moor". I told him then that I also had that feeling at Stoney Cross and no longer fished there at night for peal. A child had drowned in the pool many years ago and was commemorated by the rough stone cross erected by her parents. Will, the keeper, had told me of the tragedy which had happened before his time. The child often played by the water, he had heard, and trapped the fingerling trout in the little gravel pools. It was not known how the accident came about as no one else was there, but the older women of the village said she was a happy, joyous child. And this she must have been for the pool by day, for me and for the birds and animals which eat and drink close by, is a beautiful, wild and yet a gentle resting place.

The River Keeper and the
Blue Coated Mink

A S DUSK FELL AT SIX O'CLOCK in the evening of 28th February Fareye the buzzard courted his mate high in the clear blue sky. His wings held him above the wooded valley of the river without the expenditure of energy, for he was supported by an air current forced up as the north wind hit the valley side. His mate flirted with him as they rose and fell, with the eye of the wind their compass and source of energy. A single star shone momentarily, blinked, then shone more brightly as the pair arrowed their wings and swooped earthward in free fall to the roost in the great wood.

Two pink and sparkling eyes watched the display without fear. Bluecoat, for that was the colour of his pelt, feared little other than man and dogs; he did not fear Fareye who had once made the mistake of dropping on him with spread talons. It had happened two years previously when he had been playing on the river bank. About to follow his brown sisters down the stream, a rush of wind caused him to look up, bare his teeth and chitter in rage at Fareye who beat clumsily and heavily to check his swoop, fearful of the angry little animal who jumped and bit his scaly yellow leg. The mink dropped off, leaving the bird to fly away with two red blood drops on his left foot,

Forgetting the buzzards, Bluecoat continued on his way down the river. He travelled close to the water looking for a small animal or fish to catch, his course as much in the river as on the bank. He could submerge for two minutes without discomfort to examine the underwater roots of the waterside trees where he searched for trout and frogs. His mind was only half on food for early spring was the time of courtship and he sought a mate. He had a territory of one and a half miles which he patrolled to keep away travelling male mink lacking a ground of their own. He did not have much trouble with them for he was that which, in Devon, would be described as a 'master' mink. Fully thirty inches from the tip of his tail to the end of his nose, he weighed four pounds, and few rivals cared to dispute his stretch of the river.

Will the water keeper was aware of Bluecoat, intending to trap him for his pelt, but had decided to await November when the coat would be in top condition. Will supplemented his wages each winter in this manner as the fur buyer paid handsomely for animals in good condition.

Will, like Bluecoat, lived alone. A tall, thin, bony man, he did for himself in so sketchy a manner that the meagre diet accounted for his angular structure. His nose was aquiline, face thin, eyes blue and his cheeks fought hard to sustain a little pinkness in the general pallor of his countenance. Will was not a good 'manager', largely due to his liking for beer. He rarely bought replacement clothes and when he did the jackets had sleeves which were too short and exposed his bony wrists. His hands were also

bony, with long tapering fingers which terminated in chipped nails. His legs were covered by old grey flannel trousers from a second hand shop and these disappeared into the tops of cracked black gumboots. He wore no hat, his wispy mouse-coloured hair blowing about in the moorland wind. In winter there was usually a drop on the end of his nose.

The water keeper lived in an estate cottage on the moor. The outside was whitewashed and the roof tiled with slates—Will having no wife, his cottage would be one of the last to be modernised, there being no electricity. The front door, which faced the river, led into a short passage with the single living room on the right, back door to the wood shed ahead and the stairs to the left led to a single bedroom. It was a long time since the inside of the cottage had been painted. In the centre of the living room was a table covered with a worn oil cloth upon which was an oil lamp and the remains of Will's last meal. Two wooden chairs were by the table and an elm Windsor chair, his grandfather's, was drawn up to the range which he lit in the coldest weather or when he wanted to heat water in kettles for a bath in the tub kept in the shed. There was an oil stove on which he cooked his meals in summer. On the granite block which surmounted the opening for the range and chimney was a cuckoo clock—the fact that it did not work worried him not at all for he told the time by the light of day or the portable radio which he had bought five years ago in 1956. He sometimes listened to the news and the goings on in the outside world of those Chancellor boogers who fixed the price of beer and tobacco, but mostly he forgot to replace the run-down batteries and had to reply on the gossip in the public bar of the Poundsworthy Inn.

Will, who ate little, drank much beer in the evening to assuage loneliness and I for one enjoyed his company. "You'm welcome to our county m'dear," he said to me one May evening as we sat on high stools in the dimness of the bar. "Zum do say that ee be fishing wi' worms." Fly only was the rule on the river and I had just caught two salmon, to the well concealed envy of the locals. "But us do know m'dear, that ee be a proper gennulman an' fish wi' feathery flies." Having my skill thus tactfully acknowledged to soften the insult of suspicion, he downed another pint before enquiring whether it was true, as he had heard, that I greased my fly line. Feeling that this was becoming too technical for the time of night I produced two low water salmon flies as a gift and remarked that they were the killing patterns. "Cor-booger," croaked Will, "them little flippity flies". His Adam's Apple bobbed up and down and I could see that, although for the sake of our friendship sealed over some years he wanted to believe me, a doubt nevertheless persisted. I went to bed upstairs in the pub to fall asleep on the sagging mattress. My feet touched the foot board of the bed and my knees had to be bent for I am over six foot; it was clear that the bed belonged to that era when many of the Devon males were five foot six inches or less—was I not daily reminded of this as I cracked my skull in a doorway. "Bliddy diddy men they must 'a been in the county in the nineteenth century," remarked a builder in Tavistock.

Bluecoat was not sleeping. He was hungry—sometimes he was able to find frogs as they 'burped' their mating calls in the muddy places, but tonight they were silent. A mallard duck sat tight in the rough grass on her feather-lined nest in which clustered ten grey/green eggs—if she kept still and her feathers tight closed the mink might not smell her. Bluecoat passed on, left the river and followed a hedge up the hill to a farm where he killed two ducklings. On the way back to the river he sucked the blood of a sickly lamb leaving two tooth marks as evidence. Dick, the farmer, swore to be revenged when he found the ailing lamb and told Will he ought to be about his business caring for the river and trapping pests, instead of swallowing more ale than was good for him. Will kept his counsel and waited for the winter trapping season.

We met by the water again in September, Bluecoat, Will and myself. I was casting a Thunder and Lightning salmon fly into a full river on a wet day when the keeper appeared silently at my side. You never saw him come or heard him arrive, for he was part of the moor in the old tweed jacket. He took my rod to move away downstream, jumping from rock to rock in his gumboots, false casting in the air as he moved to catch the feel of the twelve-foot salmon rod. Finally he stopped behind a blackthorn bush at the side of the river and, without pausing, dropped my fly into the top of a short deep narrow run. After three casts a black head came up, the rod bent and a salmon thrashed momentarily on the surface as Will drove home the hook. He came out from behind the bush and moved down below the salmon, keeping the rod held high. "A master fish, m'dear," he shouted excitedly as the salmon leaped, showing its red autumn colours. "A bit red but he'll cut alright". I waited, silent and still with the net in a slack backwater until Will achieved dominance and brought the salmon down to me. I scooped out the fish and thumped the life from him with one blow to the back of the skull with a piece of metal pipe. He gave me the fish as I slipped a five pound note into his pocket—hoping it wouldn't fall out of the inevitable hole in the bottom.

I pulled a piece of cord out of my jacket, threaded it through the salmon's gills, out of his mouth, hitched it around the wrist of the broad tail and tied the two ends together to make a carrying handle. We walked on down the river towards the pub, watched by Bluecoat who scampered down the far bank, excited by the smell of fish carried to him by the east wind blowing up the river. "That mink be turrible cheeky," observed Will, who really regarded all the animals, birds, sheep and ponies of the moor as his friends. He had never yet been known to report anyone fishing without a licence, contenting himself with admonishing the wrongdoer. He probably had a fellow feeling for his victim as he himself made unauthorised visits to forbidden waters from time to time when the owners were believed to be absent. The mink ran down the bank, slid into the river and swam away between some boulders.

I returned to my home in Dorset, where I was living in those years, thinking Will would deal with the mink in the trapping season. When November came with the first frosts I watched the white barn owl quartering the ground outside my window on soft floating wings, alighting on a fence post fifty yards away to survey his hunting territory. The owl roosted in a cob barn two miles away. His pellets of mouse bones and fur littered the earth floor and his offspring hunted in the nearby St. James and Wildhampton water meadows. Snipe fed in the soft mud close to the stream at the bottom of the garden. In March I spun for pike in the Dorset Stour and cut them to feed the cats. The days lengthened, the rooks repaired their nests and a thrush laid the first blue egg in her mud-lined nest close to the garden gate.

In April my thoughts returned to Devon and after the first heavy rains I was on my way in the old red Ford. Over the Stour at Blandford, the Piddle and Frome, Axe, Otter, Teign, all were crossed with a glance to see the water. A black cat crossed the road ahead—that should be good for a fish—buzzards in the sky, a dead badger at the roadside, night victim of a passing car with blinding lights, as were the hedgehog casualties. Breakfast at the Poundsworthy where I purchased a rod licence, and then went off to the river. It was a cold wet April day which, by afternoon, chilled my fingers to white sticks. I fished on down a long pool without result but backing up the water the fly swept in a curving swim across as a salmon 'head and tailed' at the Hairy Mary fly. Ten minutes later I straightened my back with a grunt after landing the salmon, to see Bluecoat watching from the other bank. Far from becoming part of a fur coat in the recent winter he was very much alive.

Will explained the matter when I called on him for a cup of tea in his cottage. He had dug his cage trap into the river bank one afternoon, hiding it with the mouth close to the water level in a bay which Bluecoat frequented: in the bag of the cage he tied two herrings' heads. The next morning the pressure plate on the cage floor had sprung the trap door, but this had failed to close due to a dislodged stone. "An' do ee know m'dear, th' booger took the fish aids [heads] with un".

Well, that was what Will told me, but he looked sheepish and it is my belief he let the bluecoat go.

The Specimen Trout

THE BOY FELT THE SUNNY light of early morning from behind his eyelids. He opened them as he lay relaxed and warm to look at the blue sky beyond the bedroom window, whilst contentment spread through his limbs for today he would go fishing. There were two weeks ahead of him, a length of time which could at first be squandered; towards the end he savoured every daylight hour. He respected the trout fishing knowledge of his grandfather with whom he spent the holiday on the edge of the moor. Grandpa rarely called him Giles, just 'boy'. "Now boy," he would say at breakfast, "which stream will you fish today?" The old man had not left the zeal of youth behind in his journey through life, and as the boy unfolded the plan for the day the grandfather could see it all come true: the red spots on the flanks of the little moorland trout the boy would catch; the Blue Upright fly dancing down towards him on the rippling stream. He felt again the temptation of the wriggling worm which could be kicked from under a dried up cowpat. Grandpa knew that Giles considered him old, but to himself his years had passed too quickly for him to feel his age.

Giles hid his bicycle behind a stone wall in the shade of a sycamore tree. It was not a good day for fishing, being hot with a hint of thunder in the air; he was glad to have completed the six miles to the stream. He untied his rod from the crossbar of his bike, pulled it out of the cloth sleeve and assembled the two sections. The rod was fibreglass of eight feet six inches in length, his first proper trout rod. He had hoped for a split cane like Grandpa's but the old man said he would have to wait a bit. Giles knew that only wealthy families like Wilberforce's at school, old generals, retired colonels, fishing doctors and senior gentlemen owned split cane—perhaps one day...He was in any case proud of his rod which was a Christmas present. The reel and line had been purchased from a tackle shop where the man in charge had said he ought to have a net and fly box. His father, who did not fish, added these to the outfit. The net had a wooden handle two feet long and arms which flicked up to extend the meshed bag: it was neither expensive nor foolproof as the meshes at times caught in the spreading arms and the whole would become jammed in a half open position. The fly box was heavy, being of tin painted black; beneath the single lid were compartments for the flies. Wilberforce had an expensive silver coloured box of polished aluminium; the flies were enclosed in little compartments with individual transparent lids which sprang open at the touch of a finger. The box was flourished with some ostentation at the waterside.

Giles ran the line through the rings of the rod, the reel clicking sweetly as it unwound. He attached a 5X leader to the line and tied a small Blue Upright to the point. Picking up his tackle and bag he walked down through the trees to the stream. It was a secluded water running off the moor and down through the woods, protected from the sun by a canopy of trees. Sunbeams cut slanting shafts through openings in the leaves to light patches of golden gravel. As he came closer to the water the boy moved with caution, making his final approach behind a bush through which he peered into the pool beyond. There were trout there but he could not see a really worthwhile fish. Six inches was the common size, eight would bring a craggy smile to Grandpa's face and could be taken to the kitchen. What he really wanted was a ten-inch fish—a specimen, as Wilberforce would say, a sizeable trout well above the six inch limit. Wilberforce had landed a twelve-incher last term of which he had been justly proud and slightly condescending as he described the capture to his friend. He, Giles, must do as well, or better, and take a photograph to prove the truth of his account. He moved up the river until he came to an old sheep dip, long disused. A stone wall ran down one side of the stream, the other wall had collapsed into the water and now made hiding places for the trout. A wren had nested in one of the crevices in May; the moss, dried leaves and horsehair lining had been pulled out and were visible to Giles as he crept up on the likely secret place. The boy watched the moving water for a long time, just his head above the bank. As he peered, the secrets of the rocks and currents were revealed and he saw The Specimen. The tail gave the fish away, for the whole of the trout looked almost black and the rocks behind were dark as well, but the tail was a little less black and it moved—very slightly. The Specimen had taken up a comfortable position in front of a rock where little swimming effort was required. He was large for the stream and there could be no doubt, as Wilberforce would say, drawing on his greater experience, that he would give a good account of himself. Giles stared; he was reluctant to do anything which might scare the fish for there was satisfaction in just looking at the powerful shape. The trout would be experienced, he could not be otherwise having lived for so long without falling victim to the heron or the otter. Any disturbance and he would disappear..."pushed off, old boy. Too heavy a Woolworth's leader I daresay" would be Wilberforce's comment: his leaders came from Farlow's of Pall Mall.

The boy backed down the bank, sat down and sought a solution. A Blue Upright would be no good—being of insufficient substance. The bait had to be something succulent and surprising, a once-in-a-month delicacy which would be washed downstream if The Specimen did not take an immediate chance. At the same time it must not be something he had never seen before or he might be frightened. The mouthful must excite a memory of a satisfying experience. Giles did not use so many words in his mind but he would know what it was when he could think of it. Then the penny dropped. A frog, a small live frog was the answer, there could be no doubt. How could a frog possibly conceal deceit? Frogs were simple succulent creatures with wide and innocent eyes. Giles found a froglet in a swampy place close by which he had visited at Easter to collect tadpoles in a jar. The baby frogs were much the same size as his thumb nail and still had a small protruding tail. He picked one up and at once felt sorry for the creature. He had to think of a way to catch the trout and, at the same time, allow the froglet to escape. The capture of The Specimen could not be marred by the death of the bait.

From his fly box Giles took his largest fly, a No. 8 Peter Ross, which Grandpa said would catch a peal. He stripped the hook of all the dressing with his knife and tied it to the end of his leader. He picked up one of the baby frogs and held it in a dock leaf in order not to discomfort the creature with his hot hand. Returning to the sheep dip the boy looked again with caution. The trout was still there, clearly watching out for food and not at all suspicious or disturbed. Giles crept away. Taking the froglet from the leaf he slipped the hook through the very end of the tail, comforting himself with the thought that the last remnant of its tadpole life would fall off soon in any case and it would swim very well that way, and probably escape when its part in the plot had been completed.

The boy pushed his rod over the edge of the sheep dip wall with his right hand, let go the bait with his left, the frog swung over the stream, dropped into the water with a plop in front of The Specimen and set off strongly with a firm breast stroke for the far side. The Specimen, clearly astonished by this foolhardy behaviour, dropped back two feet, spun round once below the frantically swimming frog and took it in a gulping swirl. The hook pierced his mouth which he hurriedly opened, the frog was ejected and, free once more, swam off. The Specimen fought hard, almost escaping when the arms of the net failed to click open but the boy, as boys do, found a sandy bay in which he beached the fish. He hit the trout on the head with part of a kitchen chair leg, his priest, gave it "the coup-de-grace, or quietus" as Wilberforce would say. The thought of his friend reminded him of the photograph and other matters, such as weight and length, which would verify the truth of the tale he would tell on his return to school.

A breathless, hot and excited boy reached his grandparent's house at tea time. "Grandpa, grandpa. Look,

look. I've got a specimen, a beauty. Do you think it can be two pounds?" Grandpa looked, and a sadness and a happiness momentarily joined in his mind that such days for him were over. "It really is a large one, perhaps a record for the stream. Where did you get him?" The story poured out in a spate of words and the old man marvelled at the unchanged ways. Not that he would want to go through life again but, for a moment he had regrets and stifled a trace of envy as he took the photograph.

On the first day of term Giles ran into school clutching the picture. The carefully prepared description of the battle with the trout, to be delivered in matter-of-fact tones, stored ready in his mind. "A two pounder" drawled the listening Wilberforce "not bad, not bad at all. By the way, take a look at this". He produced an enlarged colour photograph of himself standing before an impressive Highland river: in his arms he held a salmon.

The Torn Gill Flap

THE GREY-MUZZLED black labrador dog lay on the damp heather. His back was pressed against the circular growth rings at the end of one of the two cut tree trunks that, together with transverse planks, spanned the stream to form a foot bridge. He was content to lie there warmed by the sun of an early December day, which had melted the white frost from the ground. He was not alone. He could touch with his black nose the soles of a pair of smooth-studded, cracked, leather boots, which protruded, toes down, from under a gorse bush. The boots belonged to his owner who was also old, worn smooth by life, and whose face was cracked and crinkled like the boots. The dog accepted the fact that his leader lay under the bush because he had been before to the place where the old man did this thing: it was enough for the dog to guard his master's back. He must not go to the owner of the boots to assure him of his presence or he would be chided—his instruction was to 'lie there' and this he did.

The boots had been still for a long time; the arthritic knees above were damp; the stomach was flat on the ground the back arched upwards, propped there by wet elbows; the

156

chin, cupped in the supporting hands, was cold; the eyes, through Polaroid spectacles, cut through the water surface film into the stream. They were fixed on a pair of spawning sea trout whose tails waved over small stones and golden gravel. The cock fish was large for a peal, all of 5 lb thought the old man, and he attended a smaller hen whose silver flank shone momentarily as she arched her spine twice in an egg extruding spasm. The cock fish saw the convulsion, and the aroma of the eggs being carried into the gravel crevices by the current stimulated his purpose: moving up, he lay alongside the female, overlapping her in length at head and tail, and with a quiver his curved body expelled the fertilizing milt. The mating had been consummated many times, and after each tender, exhausting expulsion he dropped back two feet to guard the redd whilst both recovered strength. Sometimes the hen left him, swimming away out of sight of the watcher, but the cock remained.

The male fish was not worn and diseased, as were the cock salmon spawning in the stream, but the red of his gill rakes was exposed by a torn gill flap on the side nearest to the old man. The fish had been born in the stream five years before: had left as a two-year-old fingerling in spring for the sea where it had fed for five months before returning later that year to fertilize, by chance of proximity, the eggs of a hen four times his weight. He had returned to the sea after Christmas and further coastal feeding had lifted his weight to twenty ounces on his second spawning run.

On both of these visits he escaped the estuary salmon and mullet nets, for his slim body slipped through the nylon mesh, but the second encounter stripped scales in a dark rash from his silver flank. At the end of the third marine regeneration he swam high in the water along the

157

coast to the estuary of the river of his birth, entered the fresh water and ran upstream for five miles: there a poacher's gill net caught him. He did not drown, as had salmon trapped before him with their heads stuck in the mesh, for his head became jammed up to the gills a few moments before the net was drawn to the bank. The poacher grabbed the fish by the tail and in the twisting struggle a gill cover had been torn. He escaped, the wound healed, but the shortened flap no longer covered the blood-laden rakes that took oxygen from the water. The fish was marked for life.

The old man knew nothing of these adventures but he recognized the damaged fish as one had seen in other places in the stream over the past two weeks, several redds having been dug by the couple whose spawning was near completion. The toes of the boots drew at the heather roots; the elbows pushed back; the old man backed out of the hole in the gorse bush and sat on his haunches, slowly straightening his back. The movement was painful. The dog rose to rub his muzzle on the extended hand before both walked home to the stone cottage set under the hill beneath the gnarled wind-blackened beech trees of the moor.

They lived in simplicity, man and dog; no carpet warmed the slate flags of the floor; no cloth covered the pine table; and the dog's place was a basket of rush worked by a blind man in the distant town. But the cottage welcomed them as it had others within the protection of its walls over the centuries. A black cast-iron range gave out heat to a Windsor chair close to a pile of logs, and on the table stood an oil lamp beside the old man's spectacles. When he had left his house in the town, after the death of his wife, he had thought at first to install an electric generator, but the disruption of such an event put him off, and whilst considering the matter he had made do with oil lamps. In the end he bought a Tilley, by the bright light of which he tied his trout and sea trout flies—otherwise he used the lamps which were silent and gave out a warming glow. The range was set back in a fireplace surmounted by a granite slab on which were a badger's skull, a pair of binoculars, and a jar of spills to light the lamps. Above the mantelpiece hung an oil painting of a woman fishing a moorland stream. A row of fishing rods hung from nails driven into a strip of wood along one wall, a line dryer from the bygone age of silk rested on top of a dresser by some plates, and a trout net was propped against the wall. Books, large and small, leather-bound and cloth-covered, together with a portable radio were on the table. The plastered walls were relieved by water-colours of birds—snipe, duck, geese and an oil of curlews flighting at dawn to estuary sand bars uncovered by the tide. The old man looked about and took comfort from his things.

He fed the dog. Ladling biscuit with a tin mug from a paper sack into a milk churn lid he added half a tin of meat and a soaking of milk from the can he collected daily from the farm. The dog ate to one side of the room whilst the old man warmed his knees before the opened door of the stove which glowed behind the bars. Later he also ate: a meal of pigeon he had shot flighting in to roost earlier in the week, a baked potato which had cooked during his absence and some sprouts—all washed down by a glass of red wine from the town, which he visited on pension day, driving there in a battered Land Rover with the dog on a sack in the back.

After his meal he carried the dishes through into the scullery, worked the handle of the pump which drew water from the well and washed up, warming the cold water with a dousing from the kettle on the range. Settling himself in the chair, the wine to hand, he turned on the news and then reached over and tapped the barometer. Rain would come he thought, out of the west, for a wind was moving over the moor and the clouds had lowered as he walked home. He turned off the radio and reached for a book as the patter of the first drops touched the windows. For a while he read until his chin fell forward and he slept. Later, in the darkness of the bedroom, he heard the drumming of the rainstorm on the roof.

The level rose rapidly in the stream as the rain ran from the hills; the flow coloured, white froth formed in the pockets under the peat banks and the last of the autumn leaves from the beech trees were carried away downstream. The sea trout with the damaged gill went with them. Slipping out of the stream into the river he worked his way down the valley, pool by pool, over the weirs and through the salmon ladders until he reached the gentler waters winding through the lowland farms. He came at last to the weir that divided the river from the salt waters of the sea. He was of the river and of the sea: the one his nursery, the other healed his spawning sores and gave him food. The sea accepted him, absorbing without acknowledgement the return of its foster child from the river that gave the fishes birth. For nine months he swam and fed in the ocean paths. His pale, softened flesh deepened in colour, his flanks hardened, his muscles were tuned for an August river entry as he swung north up the estuary that had welcomed him before. He settled below the weir in company with three grilse and several smaller peal that made their way upstream in the night. For seven days and nights he waited with the grilse, pestered by the hooks and leads of small boys who cast worms into the pool. In the second week thunder rolled over the moor, lightning cut the sky and grey sheets of rain drifted down to fill the runnels, the brooks, the upland river—and then the water rose over the weir. Momentarily the fish was visible as he leaped and then he was swallowed by the dark water above the sill.

The old man had fished for trout in the summer. Watched by the dog he cast his Wickham's Fancy up ahead and struck sharply when a brownie dimpled at the fly. Small as they were he ate the trout and the magpies picked over the skins and heads he scraped off the plate onto the garden wall. He no longer fished for salmon—there was no point for he could not eat so large a fish and there was no need to sell. But sea trout, particularly the small ones— they were a different matter. He loved a sea trout. He sat at the table in his cottage as the rain came down: in front of him was a fly-tying vice with a No. 8 hook in the jaws. The old man looked at the hook, which he had placed there by habit, forming in his mind the kind of fly he would make to suit the water when he fished in two nights' time. The spate in the river would have run away by then, but a little colour would remain and there would be fresh peal in the tails of the pools. A large fly? Yes, he ought to dress an offering of substance to match the stained water. He removed the No. 8 and clamped tight on a No. 4. The dressing was plain: a silver body, a teal wing and black varnish for the head. He tied another—just in case he lost the first. They were good flies with no fancy trimmings—he stroked their points on the flat of an oil stone and tested them on the nail of his thumb.

Two evenings later he sat on a stone by the river, waiting for the light to fade. The chosen pool darkened in front of him, bats swerved over the surface as they hawked for flies, and a rabbit, caught by a stoat, squealed on the far bank. All became quiet. The dog also watched the water and tested the wind of night. They had seen peal jump, and a salmon had leaped once to bash down with a crash which sent waves lapping under the bank beneath their feet. A lightening to the east gave notice of a moon. The old man rose; the time had come. He picked up the rod, retrieved the fly and leader from the pool where they had been soaking, and drawing line from the reel cast out towards the break in the smooth

water where the glide ran out into the stickle below. On the third cast the line straightened, there was a flurry of white spray in the shallows as a small peal took the fly. The short fight was followed by surrender—he drew the fish across the surface and beached it on the shingle at his feet. He tapped the one-pound sea trout on the head, removed the hook and tossed the fish to the dog, which carried it to the stone where he had left his bag.

The moon rose above the hill, shining directly into his eyes and in reflection from a path of brightness on the water. He waded out to cast square across into the avenue of light, the fly pitched in and was taken within two yards in the deep water below the bushes on the opposite bank. For a moment all was still, his hands felt for information, his eyes searched for the line, which moved with increasing speed to the head of the pool where a sea trout leaped twice with awesome crashes—then all went slack. The old man stripped in fast, drawing the yards in over his finger, his heart sank and then, below him, the water bulged as the sea trout turned, then moved up level with his legs. The dog came to the shingle bank as the old man backed out of the water when the sea trout showed a silver side. The beaching was gentle, a push from behind and there he lay on his side, the damaged gill flap visible in the light of the harvest moon.

The old man removed the hook, wet his hands, turned the fish to the river of nativity and slid him away. The sea trout wallowed, righted itself and faded from sight with a stroke of the square tail. The old man, who could not eat so large a fish, lifted his hat an inch and murmured 'We'll meet again, by the foot bridge, in December.'

The Flyfishing Macnab

H E WOULD BE ALLOWED to fish from one hour before sunrise until one hour after sunset on one day in the month of June. In that period of about sixteen hours he had to catch, net and release one salmon, and catch and be allowed to keep a wild brown trout and a sea trout. He could fish any fly he chose, and vary the patterns as conditions dictated. If he failed he had to dress six Copper Dart salmon tube flies for his friend. Ernest knew that Mike considered the flies as good as his because the river was low and clear and all the salmon were stale and torpid.

The trout, he knew, would not be a problem as the river in the higher reaches was full of the little beggars. The salmon and sea trout were a different matter as the only real chance at a salmon was after rain, and the sea trout hardly moved until after dark. Ernest did not want to dress those flies as they needed jungle cock eyes and the JC cape he had was plucked almost bare.

Deep in thought as he evolved a plan he walked along the river bank at dusk to the fishing hut. With a torch between his teeth he undid the two padlocks securing the top and the lower doors of the old shepherd's hut and climbed inside. The interior was still warm after the heat of the summer day. He struck a match and lit the stump of a candle on the bench and at once turned his attention to the record book which showed a 3 ½ lb peal caught and released the night before but in, for him, forbidden time. He read: "21 June. 3 ½ lb retd. Luke. Above the dam. Stale. 1" Alex tube. 11.30 pm. Water low and clear. Warm. ½ waxing moon".

He put down his rucksack and took out two lamb chops, a packet of potato chips and a bottle of claret, together with his camera complete with flash to substantiate his catch. Lighting the stove he prepared and ate his supper whilst seated on a stool at the record book bench. It was very satisfactory to be in the quiet and peace of the late evening and drink a glass of wine. He glanced about the hut at the paper cutout of a monster 11 lb sea trout, and at the paper description of an angler:

"Behold the fisherman. He riseth early in the morning and disturbeth the whole household. Mighty are the preparations, and he goeth forth full of hope. When the day is far spent he returneth smelling of strong drink, and the truth is not in him".

On one wall were weighing scales calebrated to 15 lbs, a trout net, a Gye net for salmon and a sea trout net with the rim painted white to be visible in the dark.

Ernest poured himself another glass of wine and going outside sat on a tree stump by the river. An owl hooted and a sea trout jumped and splashed down on the water to send waves across the pool. The last rays of the sun sank below the horizon to his rear. This would be close to the time when he would normally start to fish for sea trout, but he had decided to rest the river all through the night and go for the salmon one hour before sunrise. He set about his preparations: from the rack in the hut he took down his 12 ft salmon fly rod, attached a 9 ft length of 10 lb nylon to the point of the floating fly line and knotted on a No. 12 Thunder & Lightning low water barbless single hook fly. He propped the rod against a fork in a bankside tree ready for the first light of the morning. Going back into the hut he unrolled his sleeping bag on the camp bed, set the alarm clock for 0244 hrs, being two hours before sunrise, folded his jacket as a pillow and lay down facing the open door of the hut. He thought of the shepherd who used to live in the hut for a month in the fields at lambing time, and of the coke stove he would have lit to warm himself in the March nights. He watched through the open door as the moon sank down below the hills to the west. As he drifted into sleep he heard the squeak of a bitch otter as she called her cubs.

It was still fully dark when the alarm went off. He lit the candle, boiled the kettle on the stove, made some tea and ate two biscuits. Going outside he pulled on his thigh boots, slung the Gye net over his head onto his back, reset the alarm for 0344 hrs when he could start to fish, and together with the camera, walked with purpose to the river.

He was already wading and waiting when the reset alarm went off on the bank and he made his first cast straight across the pool. Dawn was the only chance for a salmon under the prevailing conditions. He believed this to be true as he had heard someone say a cast before dawn was a racing certainty, and he knew his friend Mike often took peal at that time. Even so, he was startled when the line tightened into a fish at his third cast. Would it be a sea trout or a salmon? If a sea trout he might as well go home and start dressing the six Copper Dart flies as there would be no chance of a salmon after the disturbance of landing this fish which was, he felt, large, for it would soon be daylight. For ten minutes the fish sulked close to the river bed, made one or two short runs and was netted. He felt there was hope as the fish behaved too dully for a big peal. Holding the net with the fish underwater he examined the tail—it was concave—a salmon! Ernest reached for the flash camera, hung his watch on the landing net handle beside the salmon's tail and took two shots at 0410 hrs. He tweaked free the hook and sank the net. Released, the salmon wobbled, then slid away in the dark water. Ernest sat, breathless and shaking on the bank, then went back to the hut, lay down and fell asleep.

It was mid-day when he drove from Hut Pool on the lower river where he had caught the salmon, to the finger streams of the high moor near his home to gather some trout for his supper. It was not a good fishing day, being hot with a bright sun. Even so, by tea time he had a creel of four, none above eight ounces in weight. He had fished a No. 16 hackled Kite's Imperial and struck when the little fellows dimpled at the fly. Cleaned, they revealed a varied diet of stonefly creepers, caddis larvae and unidentified half digested insects. Satisfied, as he took the photograph, he thought the Copper Darts were more than half saved.

Back at the hut he drank a tin of beer, ate the trout and planned the evening ahead. Sunset, the calendar noted, would be at 2122 hrs, so 2222 hrs would be the cut-off time for the Macnab. He planned a possible route to success: at 2145 hrs he would fish through the pool with a floating line, 6 lb leader and a medium-sized Pot Bellied Pig with No. 12 outpoint treble. Thereafter, if not successful, he would skim a surface lure.

He set up two rods for the two methods as there would be no spare minutes to change tackle if the Pot Bellied Pig failed. He then sat on the bank close to the water and looked hopefully at the sky for the first stars; none were visible at 2140 hrs but he could wait no longer. Picking up the Pig he slid gently into the river making neither splash, ripple nor noise. The line snaked across the water, the fly plopped in and Ernest retrieved the line in gentle draws over his index finger. After ten minutes he had fished halfway down the pool when a sea trout took, bent the rod over, jumped, took off down the pool and came off. He waded ashore, put down the rod, picked up the surface lure outfit and started to back-up the pool with the Yellow Dolly which arrowed across the dark placid surface. At 2215 hrs a cavernous pair of jaws opened and smacked shut on the Dolly and the fish set off for the tail of the pool and the sea. Ernest followed, rod held high and thigh boots full. After thirty yards of wading he hauled out onto the bank, resolved to give no more line as he had long been on the backing. In time the peal came back and, exhausted, showed a silver side on the dark water. Ernest netted the fish, knocked it on the head and looked at his watch, 2227 hrs, five minutes over time. Should he turn his watch back before taking the photograph? No, he would not be like the angler's description 'and the truth was not in him'. He thrust temptation aside and took the photograph with the watch draped over the rounded muscular flank of the sea trout and in front of the broad square tail. At that moment a voice came out of the night, "2227 hrs, but you hooked him at 2217 hrs, I was watching. Call it a draw". Mike loomed up out of the night. "Dress me three Copper Darts and I'll give you just the main course". Off they went to the pub, and whether they returned smelling of strong drink is not for me to say.

Lightning Source UK Ltd.
Milton Keynes UK
21 August 2010

158785UK00001B/14/P